Revelations in the d'Arc

Revelations © Copyright 2003 Kenane Barlow and Anna De Feo

Cover design: © Anna De Feo and Kenane Barlow, based on a photograph by Anna De Feo taken at the cathedral at Poissy.

All rights reserved. No part of this work may be reproduced or stored in an information retrieval system (other than for purposes of review) without prior written permission by the copyright holder.

A catalogue record of this book is available from the British Library

First Edition: September 2003

ISBN: 1-84375-043-0

United States Library of Congress: TXu 1-065-853

This is a work of fiction. Names, characters, places and incidents are the product of the author's imagination or are used fictitiously, and any resemblance to any actual persons, living or dead, events, or locales is entirely coincidental.

To order additional copies of this book please visit: http://www.upso.co.uk/revelations.htm

Published by: UPSO Ltd
5 Stirling Road, Castleham Business Park,
St Leonards-on-Sea, East Sussex TN38 9NW UK
Tel: +44 (0)1424 853349 Fax: +44 (0)870 191 3991
Email: info@upso.co.uk   Web: http://www.upso.co.uk

Revelations in the d'Arc
...a medieval midwife's tale...

---

*This story is a work of fiction.
Real events of history and real characters from history
are intertwined in our story.*

*We dedicate our work to our loving husbands,
Peter Barlow, and Joseph De Feo,
respectively, and also to our children.*

By Kenane Barlow and Anna De Feo

**Copyright 2002: TXu 1-065-853
United States Library of Congress**

All rights reserved.

*We gratefully acknowledge
Pierre and Jacqueline de Sermoise,
for their inspiration and their encouragement
in this endeavour.*

*Pierre de Sermoise
'Je suis très content d'être votre inspiration…'*

à Anna De Feu Kenane Barlow,
avec mon très amical
et respectueux hommage

Pierre de Sermoise

*Pierre and Jacqueline de Sermoise
Paris, April 2000*

'The Crown of France could be lost by the Treachery of a Whore, but saved by a Virgin...."

*The Monk Bede,
7th Century*

BOOK I

Catharine:

Cathar Ways

Chapter I

Catharine and Marie la Lapine

- 2:00 AM -

*Our Father, who art in heaven.
Hallowed be Thy Name.
Thy kingdom come.
Thy Will be done on earth,
As it is in heaven.
Give us this day our daily bread;
And forgive us our trespasses,
as we forgive those who trespass against us.
And lead us not into temptation
But deliver us from evil.
Amen.*

I was awakened by an odd musty scent filling my nostrils. It was the odour I remembered from my childhood, when I would descend into my grandmother's basement, and feel the secret intrigues that the house must have known from generations past. I sat bolt upright, both drawn by this smell and disoriented by such an unaccustomed occurrence here in my bedroom. Then I saw her.

She was a Spirit, in the figure of a large woman clothed in a long grey tunic. She wore a cape with a hood, dressed as if she were coming in from the cold. She moved silently and gracefully, removing her hood in preparation for a long visit. Even in the semi-darkness of my room, I could see her face, which she revealed as she removed her outer garment: she had a kindly face, ageless, but lined with a troubled past. She settled herself most insistently on my bed, determined that I would be her scribe. And so I am.

The corners of her lips moved up into a smile, and she began to speak, the words echoing in my head, as if they came from deep inside me. She said, '*je suis Catharine la Lapine*. I have an important tale to tell, one that changed the face of France and England, at a time when the Church was itself divided. I have carried this burden within me for over five centuries. I can no longer bear it; the truth has been veiled by the myth of time. You have correctly understood that I am a Spirit, one from France of long ago, a time when women were silently powerful in matters of State, Life and Death. Women were strong in Virtue and in Sin. Despite these powers, the world was ruled by delinquent men. But I am getting ahead of myself.

'In 1380 I was born in Carcassone, a small walled, well-defended city, in the south of France. There were two tall, forbidding towers, standing like strong sentinels many meters high, and very thick at the base, which guarded the drawbridge that provided access to the city. Once inside the city, there were winding cobbled lanes bordered by half-timbered houses.

'We lived in one of these houses, which also contained the small apothecary shop that my parents owned. They sold coarse wine, olive oil, and vinegar, as well as plants and herbs, gathered from the surrounding countryside. My mother grew special plants on a small plot of land behind the shop: mandrake, beautiful large poppies in white and red, henbane, belladonna, camomile, lavender, geraniums, and roses. Some of these plants were used in preparations to cure the sick;

occasionally potions were prepared to heal broken hearts. There was a linden tree which blossomed with fragrant little yellow flowers that would burst open, giving us the most delicious sugary petals. Occasionally my mother gave me a few of these to taste, to calm my exuberance. Ordinarily they were dried and stored for use as a calming tea.

'I was a happy little girl of five, following my mother like her diminutive shadow. She loved my constant chatter, and my endless questions about all the plants around us, even about the crickets that played their tunes throughout the summer. I watched and absorbed; she toiled with the magic preparation of the healing elixirs. Even today, when I inhale the perfume of lavender or the scent of geranium, my childhood memories flood over me. I remember my mother's cooling touch as she washed my face with a flannel immersed in rosewater.

Childhood memories are meant to be safe; my mother's chosen vocation was anything but safe, however. It was not just the work of being an apothecary that consumed her; she was quite obsessed with healing, as was my grandmother before her. My grandmother was a true Cathar; she taught my mother all her techniques. The Cathars, a Christian sect that the Church could not hold, were ever present, but hidden.

We Cathars were, I believe, truly 'loved by God' although the formal Church viewed us as heretics for our beliefs and for our miraculous use of herbal preparations. The highest level within the Cathar belief was that of the *Parfait*, one who sought perfection. Becoming a *Parfait* required an oath of Consolamentum: in preparation all sexual contact was denounced and vegetarianism adopted. The Cathar *Parfaits* lived as nomads; they had no families or possessions. They believed in the duality of life, the one side being the good, which was spiritual, and the other the bad which was largely in the realm of the physical. They believed that the satisfaction of all physical desires was evil, and subject to compliance with Satan. They believed that the way of life followed by the corrupt priests of our day clearly fit into the bad. They lived in the certainty that their own rewards would be in the next life, and that their purpose here on earth was to serve those who needed them. They knew very well the powers of herbs and roots, and sought to heal the sick. They quietly gave of themselves and required no reward. They were the healers; amongst them were midwives.

The early Church was not bothered by their presence; since they sought only to promote the highest moral and aesthetic standards; their behaviour was no threat to the Church. They were very pure. They did not live in convents as did the nuns, or in monasteries as did the monks, although they secretly maintained contact with some of those in the cloisters so that their sick could be further cared for by the Holy sisters and brothers. They often travelled on pilgrimages, wandering from place to place with the friars. They had no Church building of their own, but often took refuge within the body of the Church. They met when they could in the homes of the Faithful. The view that the Cathars were heretics varied by location; they were tolerated in Carcassone where we lived, and also in most of the Languedoc region. In other areas, when people might have visions – or perhaps delusions, often brought about by some of the herbal preparations – then both the individuals and the Cathars themselves would be accused of spiritual impurity or of possession by the devil. In these times, accusation was equivalent to judgement. And judgement was equivalent to torture and death, death not only of the body but of the eternal Spirit.

The *'Parfaits'* lived moral and exemplary lives. They and some of their Cathar followers renounced all aspects of the physical world. A small number of Cathars chose this vocation; most Cathars became *Parfaits* just before death. It was true that nuns and priests took vows of poverty, chastity, and obedience: the Cathar *Parfaits*, however, lived these vows. They refused to eat meat, cheese, milk, and eggs, as they felt that these products were the result of animal intercourse, the purpose of which was to give life to fellow creatures.

My mother was their chief supplier in Carcassonne. I remember Pierre de Mirepoix, the *Parfait*, who often came to the shop. He always had time to share a moment with me.

'*Catharine, ma petite,*' he would say, 'if ever you see a small creature suffering by the wayside, lay a hand on him, you have the gift of healing in your little hands...' and then he would tell me stories:

'I must sing you an extraordinary ditty, Catharine, about a time when our faith was being destroyed by King Philippe the Fair. There was a man who sang a song in Foix, which was a town, not very far from here, where many of us lived. This is how it goes:

> *Il était une fois (Foi)*
> *un bonhomme de Foix (Foi)*
> *qui vendait du foie (Foi)*
> *dans la ville de Foix (Foi).*
> *Il a dit 'Ma Foi!*
> *c'est la dernière fois (Foi)*
> *que je vend du foie (Foi)*
> *dans la ville de Foix (Foi)*
> *Ma Foi !'*

Yes, my Catharine, you must not forget this little song; it is how the French of the future, will be taught that *fois/foi/foie/Foix* is spelled in different ways. And although it seems to be a silly little song about a man selling liver, the real message is that there was one Faith in the town of Foix and a man of Faith cried the warning that it would be the last time he would declare his Faith. His Faith was our Faith, which will endure to the end of time.'

'What is spelling, Pierre de Mirepoix?'

'Ah, Catharine, you will learn, you will learn. For now, just remember these few words.'

'You should remember Foix – a very important town. It was the last place where the Church tried to destroy our Faith. But we know that it is with us, silently and secretly protecting all of us, always.'

'And now I must have a word with your *Maman*.'

'Marie, I have many who are grievously ill, suffering from the 'Bobo[1]'. I know I cannot heal them, just ease their suffering and give them peace. Some of your most powerful mandrake, please, and also some lavender and almond oil.' He paid for his purchases, although my mother never asked a specific sum, and departed, only to reappear the next day, and to tell me again the story of the man of Faith.

That is why I remember it so well.

=================

Despite the obvious security of the city of Carcassone, there was a prevailing undercurrent of fear. I expect that this feeling was related to what was the accepted behaviour and the sympathy – or rather the empathy and oneness - we felt as a part of our discrete Cathar community. My mother told me where to walk for safety, as there were many tales of murders that had been committed within these city walls. She taught me always to say the 'Our Father' when I was afraid, as none could argue with those words. They would protect me. We tried to fade into the background and not be noticed. We maintained our silence.

It was in May of this year, 1385, I am certain, that Pierre de Mirepoix came again, soon after, and whispered words to my mother. 'Marie, I come today to warn you. We hear that the *ecorcheurs*[2] are approaching our area. They are attacking isolated villages and little hamlets. They take shelter in buildings, laying empty after their residents have suffered and died of the Plague. Even small bands of Pilgrims have been set upon. They are without resources and are therefore desperate.

---

[1] Raised nodules under the arms and in the groin area which were symptomatic of the Bubonic Plague.
[2] Marauding brigands returning from military conflicts.

They behave as though they are entitled to the goods of others, as their booty. They kill the men, and rape the women, keeping them or killing them afterwards, depending upon their need. They often carry off the girls – of all ages - to use and abuse them. You, Marie, are vulnerable. You and your family must leave now. I must go, I have others to advise.'

My mother heeded him; she rushed across the room to tell my father. My father refused to believe the warning. 'We've had such warnings before,' he said. 'We are safe here, we always have been.'

I ran out of the shop, frightened by the little of the message I understood. Suddenly I heard loud shouting and the sound of approaching footsteps and the clattering of armaments, coming from the bottom of our lane. I ran back inside, to tell my mother this.

My father said, 'Marie, Catharine – I am the man – I will defend you and our home. You two go outside, climb the linden tree where you can see everything and you will be safely out of view. In a few hours time, all will be well again. When I know that they have gone, I will call you to come down.'

So my mother and I did as he said. We climbed the linden tree, and hid in the abundant foliage. We watched and wept at the scene below.

The shouting became louder. The men entered the shop. My father tried to reason with them, 'Take what you want,' we heard him say, his powerful voice resonating with compassion for their plight. 'I have no quarrel with you. I know that you suffer from the war, and have been left without support. Whatever I have, I gladly offer. I am alone here, and only ask to be left so.'

But the marauders settled themselves down in the shop and began to drink the cured wine. Based on the sounds we heard, they got quite drunk, and lost their reason. In the end they were also drunk on their power. They demanded not only our belongings, but also my father's blood.

We heard, with horror, all this happening. My father was

dragged outside. We saw him suffer their brutal beatings. It seemed an eternity before he succumbed. My mother placed her hand over my mouth to keep me quiet. Then she pressed my head to her breast and surrounded me with her body, so that I would not be witness to the violence of my father's death. I felt my mother's heart beat fast, and although she made no sound, her warm tears wet my hair like summer rain.

They packed what they wanted, and then set the shop and our home alight, and moved on. The flames spread quickly, feeding on the alcohol from the exploding casks, and the dried herbs. Our strong house which had seen so much joy crumbled into a heap, as the light of the flames flickered in my mother's eyes. When the flames had consumed all the timber and left only the scorched stones standing, we released ourselves from our locked position and painfully scrambled down from the tree. In the evening light, everything was blackened; I shall never forget the acrid smell that permeated my clothes and hair and hung in the air: it was the smell of sorrow.

My mother had lost her beloved husband, and I had lost my courageous father. I prayed for him to watch over us. We had no time to bury him properly. We placed his body on the smouldering timbers and created a funeral pyre. His remains were consumed by the flames and his spirit departed with the smoke.

My mother swallowed her grief; we had no time to feel; we were numb. We ran swiftly to the shelter which was the hidden sanctuary of Pierre de Mirepoix. It was a cave in the foothills of Carcassone.

I remember this day very clearly. I went from a life of innocence to a life of fear. I lost all the songs I knew. I could hardly speak. I began to stutter. I clung to my mother, who was so brave. Her arms protected me; I needed her. She held me and tried to make the evil events disappear. We needed a new reality.

==================

We arrived in darkness, and were greeted in silence, by Pierre de Mirepoix. He had no need to ask questions; he knew what had transpired. Most warmly and efficiently he settled us in a corner of his sanctuary. He handed us a goblet, filled with one of my mother's secret elixirs, for her to drink, and for me to sip, to ease our pain and to strengthen us. We settled and slept.

We were awakened by the dawn chorus, the songs of the birds. Pierre handed me some warm milk, and gave a cup of wine to my mother. We were given hearty crusts of bread and some nuts for breakfast. He had packed some frugal fare for us to take on our departure. For we needed to take a journey; we were seeking a new life. He gave us grey hooded loose-fitting garments to don, the traditional wear of pilgrims. He led us to a small chapel outside the walls of Carcassone where pilgrims would gather, to prepare for the next day's journey. We blended in with the others, and learnt that we would be going to Montpelier.

Chapter II

Mother Elizabeth, Montpelier

from 1385 –

*Angel of God
My Guardian dear
To whom God's love
Commits you here.*

We spent that first day of our grief preparing for our imminent journey, becoming accustomed to our new garments. I went with my mother into a field near the chapel to gather rare plants, and some herbs that we could carry with us.

I spent the night shielded by my mother's cloak, as we rested at the campfire. All around us was the singing of hymns and the unfamiliar acrid smell of strangers. We arose quite early the next day. We took our breakfast of stale bread dipped in coarse wine. Many drew their morning drink from the well, but we did not trust the water for drinking.

I was small, but I remember walking in this large group. Some would join us as we went, others would depart. We felt safe in this company, even though the travellers were very mixed. There were old and young, sick and lame, people who talked to God, and people who talked to themselves. Some frightened me, even whilst they engaged me: there were people missing limbs or bearing scars on their faces; some even had their faces half eaten away. Even wealthy people were with us; ladies travelled in covered carts drawn by the most stubborn mules. Movement had to stop when the mules decided that the grasses on the verges of the sandy lanes were particularly attractive. There was a Lady who noticed me, and heard me whining to my mother that I was tired, that my feet and my whole body ached. My mother said that she was unable to carry me, as she was herself exhausted. The Lady stopped her cart. She ordered her *charretier* to ask my mother to let me ride with her. It was the sweetest experience in this painful journey. It was truly a blessing that she was travelling the entire distance to Montpelier. From time to time, my mother was also invited to ride, a chance to rest her raw blistered feet.

As we got to know her on this journey, my mother related our tale of sorrow and our escape. She did not mention Pierre de Mirepoix, as we had to protect our true Faith and his. I had learnt to keep quiet by now, as secrets had to be treasured.

With every turn of the cart's wheel, my mother and this lady began to develop a true friendship. Their conversation became increasingly animated. I lay between them, my head on the lady's lap. The soft tones of their words consoled me like a pause in the chaos outside. The scent of incense which permeated the lady's garments soothed me. I was lulled to sleep, feeling a moment of safety at last.

Once my mother, said, 'Madame, who are you that you travel alone with such confidence?'

The lady straightened herself in her seat, smoothing the folds in her cloak, and swept her hand across her face to reveal a serene expression. She answered, 'I am a bride of Christ, I am beholden to no man, but the Son of God. I am the Prioress of the convent that is close to the University at Montpelier. I am Dame Elizabeth, the Mother Superior. By now, I am sure that you have nowhere to shelter, once we reach the town. I offer you and your daughter accommodation with me. You can join our community: you can work with us there, to contribute towards your keep. From my cart, I have seen you help countless others on this journey. Perhaps you can help us in our hospice, you seem to be blessed with a gift of healing.'

My mother was surprised. She sighed with great relief. She praised the Lord for His Guidance in finding the Answer to our prayers. In the presence of Dame Elizabeth we also began to feel confident. Some of my little tunes reappeared, in soft hums.

After travelling for what seemed to me, to be countless days, we finally approached our first view of Montpelier. The tall spire of the cathedral dominated the horizon. We made our way towards it, through meandering cobbled streets. I held tightly onto the side of the cart, jostled as the wheels lumbered over the uneven stones. The exhausted mules finally reached the gates of the Convent.

We were greeted by nuns who spoke in gentle tones. In my eyes they were the most beautiful high-born ladies, graceful in all their ways, so different from the poor and the suffering amongst our travelling companions. Dame Elizabeth explained to us that these nuns were responsible for running the convent. They also taught at the school.

There were many sisters there. Those coming from peasant or tradesmen backgrounds did the hard work. They grew the produce and tended the animals that made the convent self-sufficient. They cared for foundling children that were brought there, often left at the gate. Someone checked every morning in case any were left. Often the mothers of these children would return, seeking to care for their own children within the convent walls. In exchange for solace and shelter, they cared for the motherless babies. In reality, the arrival of babies in this way helped to perpetuate the convent: often the girls grew up to become nuns, and the boys were sent to a nearby monastery, after they reached the age of seven.

There was a large group of children at the convent when we arrived, many about my age. I found myself in a whole new world, which was serenely ordered. The torture of life as we had known it, was muffled behind the high walls. We little ones, boys and girls, were dressed in fresh-air scented clean cotton frocks in white, cream, grey, and faded navy blue. We were taught to recite prayers like little parrots, but there was a feeling of security in the rhythm of prayer. We thanked God and thanked Jesus and thanked the Holy Spirit for the succour we were receiving, the significance of which I understood all too well. We were allowed to laugh and make merry. We held hands and sang songs together. During meal times we were led into the refectory where our meals were simple, but nourishing. We enjoyed thick soups made from vegetables and oats and barley. Our hearty bread was baked in the large ovens; we soaked up the last of the soup in our bowls with a thick slice of bread.

Our lives were structured. The daily routine was dictated by the bells of the convent.

The Angelus, which to me was the call of the angels, awakened my mother and me at six o'clock in the morning. I immediately fell to my knees, and together my mother and I prayed. My mother knelt behind me and lovingly brushed my matted curls. Then my mother would dress me, and rush me out the door to please the Lord. I ran to the chapel for Matins, which seemed to last a very long time. The best part of the Mass was the singing. We actually sang in hope of our breakfast. We were little ones after all. And then, in fulfilment of our hope, it was indeed time to eat.

The day had officially begun. We were not taught to think. We were taught to do. For doing God's will would be fulfilment enough for any one of us. We learned to draw, we learned calligraphy. We learned basic literacy, but I had the advantage of learning not only from the convent school but also from my mother. We learned Latin, so that we might understand the prayers we said. Every moment was filled with providing for the necessities of this life and establishing our own store in eternity. We had many songs to learn. We prayed at least six times more each day, before meals, after meals, before Contemplation, before bedtime. We were often bewildered by the words we said, but recited them anyway, using our silent moments to think about play.

We did have moments for play, mostly planting vegetables and herbs and feeding the animals at the convent. It was my favourite time. A little cat would follow me. Her name was Mew–Mew. She was my secret friend. She lived with the cows in the stable, and slept in the hills of hay. Mew-Mew had kittens. They all became rat and mouse chasers.

Accommodation at the convent gave me a childhood sheltered from the terror of our times. Dame Elizabeth loved me as her own, for me it was almost like having a second mother or a special aunt. She also had a loving relationship with my mother, who was able to keep her informed about life outside the convent.

During the normal day, I shared very little time with my mother. She was so busy. Apart from her work in the infirmary, Dame Elizabeth provided her with access to the university at Montpelier, where she assisted by serving some of the professors, doing their cooking, cleaning, laundry and mending. In the course of working for them, she overheard them discussing new advances in medicine and healing of the sick. She gleaned insights from these conversations which complemented her own practical skills. They glibly mentioned various texts, certain that just mentioning them would impress her with their Knowledge and her own Ignorance. She, however, could read, and treasured this information, reading the referenced works as she dusted the books in the library. She won the confidence of Stephen de Foix, the most erudite of the medical professors, by accidentally sharing with him some of her practical healing skills.

Late one afternoon, in the heat of the day, whilst she was working in his chambers, he asked her for a cool drink, hoping that it would ease the pain of his headache. She first placed her hands on his forehead, which relieved his discomfort somewhat. She then prepared a solution, made from the dried flowers of the linden tree, which she always carried with her in a pouch. He drank the sweet liquid in one quick gulp. He found himself calm and drowsy, with the stress and hurt in his head evaporating nearly as quickly as he consumed the elixir. He was both bewildered and astonished by this rapid result. She was worried as she realised afterwards, that he could accuse her of being a witch, as many men fearing the unknown powers of women, might do.

But instead Stephen was wise and aware. He realised that he and my mother shared the same secret spiritual belief. He remembered his own mother placing her hands on his head in exactly the same way when he had had headaches as a child. The taste of the elixir was also familiar.

Marie wondered why she had revealed herself to this man, whom she hardly knew. Their eyes met, and it was as if she saw him for the very first time. She noticed his features: his handsome clean-shaven face, his sparkling blue eyes with their penetrating gaze, his straight nose above his full lips. For a brief moment she was transfixed: she felt her heart beating faster, the rush of warmth through her body rose to her face; she could not help but smile. She had not felt such attraction to any man since the early days of her marriage, and had not expected to feel this way again.

Stephen broke the silence. He said 'Marie, I know now who you are. You are on the path to become '*une Parfaite*'. I am on the same Path.' He took her hands in his, and gently pulled her close to him. He kissed her tired hands. She was enraptured and captivated. She had not thought of herself as someone who could be loved again until then. He continued, 'Our souls can join together on our journey; our bodies will shelter in each other on our road to perfection, if you will accept me as your lover and faithful companion. We can teach each other from the gifts we possess. In secret, I will teach you the modern methods of healing, and you will teach me how to concoct and administer the healing elixirs to diminish suffering of both body and mind.'

After this time, my mother was allowed to listen in as he rehearsed some of his discourses. Their relationship was spiritually intimate, and physically enchanting, and entirely discrete. My mother thanked God that she was able to delay becoming a *Parfaite*.

My mother returned to me every evening at the convent. One afternoon in early May when she returned from the University, she experienced a tight feeling around her heart. She described it as a feeling of foreboding, or perhaps a dark premonition. She was summoned directly to Dame Elizabeth's quarters. She closed the door behind her as she entered that stark, bare room. Elizabeth lay on her bed, without her habit, with a shawl around her greying head and shoulders. The skin on her face was transparent; her cheeks were pink with fever. Her body seemed to collapse and disappear under the sheet; she looked old for her years. The rapid change in her appearance was startling. She was moving her rosary beads methodically through her fingers. As soon as she perceived my mother's entrance, Elizabeth brightened and called her to come nearer. Her eyes looked through my mother, unable to focus on her form. She placed her hands on my mother's shoulders and whispered.

'Marie,' she said, 'I bequeath my Rosary to you.' When my mother touched it she noticed that the beads were pearls and that there was no cross on it. There was instead a golden rose. 'I am on my way... Marie, I want your blessing before I receive the Extreme Unction from our Bishop. I need not explain to you who I am and what are my beliefs. I have already sent word to Pierre de Mirepoix. He will arrive very soon. Whether you see him or not, from the moment when my eyes will be closed, you and your daughter must leave this place. Then there will be disruption here; your lives could be in danger because of your special talents. Go, take with you this letter, which is addressed to the Prioress of the Convent St Louis, at Poissy. Take also this leather pouch; the coins will ensure that you and your daughter will not go hungry on your journey. Hide it well.' Together they prayed the 'Our Father' nine times. My mother left Dame Elizabeth's quarters, distraught, after promising to abide by her counsel.

I remember this event vividly; I was nine years old. We had been in Montpelier for nearly four years. My mother awakened me directly after seeing Mother Elizabeth. She placed the Rosary around my neck, but under my clothing so that none would see. She sewed the pouch of coins into the hem of her cloak, and the missive into mine. Again we packed hastily, ready for departure the next day. She cautioned me to be silent. That was the easiest thing for me, as I had learned by now to observe and remember. I hid my sorrow, knowing that our departure was imminent. I watched her, copying her determination.

Just after breakfast, she told the nuns that she wanted to take me to the cathedral. Instead, we went to meet Stephen de Foix, and I met my mother's mentor and lover.

He greeted me with warmth, and hugged me as if I belonged to him. I was fascinated by his extraordinary blue eyes. I became aware that my mother and Stephen were one, by the way they looked at each other. My mother told him everything. Stephen then advised us how to travel northwards, through villages and hamlets, on roads and rivers. He saw that we were already distressed with this need to leave. I could see that he was afraid to let us go alone; I was grateful that he then decided to come with us. My mother was relieved; I understood that she had come to depend upon him, much as she had depended upon my father.

He spoke to me. 'Never fear, Catharine, I shall be with you, as your mother's companion and your protector, for as long as I am able. You have a lot to learn from your mother. She is very wise, and you must respect her. I know you love her, as I do. You know that you come from God, and in the end, like Dame Elizabeth, you will go to God. You will be invincible in your Faith.'

'How?' I asked, 'I am only a child, how can I be invincible? I felt the weight of my innocence to be a burden, but I was fearful of giving it up. Then he gently touched my cheek. I felt extraordinary warmth and a sensation of serenity. His touch reminded me of how my father used to stroke my cheek and comfort me.

He stood up, and returned to the table with a simple meal of bread, cheese, fruit and wine. He continued to speak to me as he broke the bread. 'Do you know the meaning of "Give us this day our daily bread", Catharine? It is not only the bread of sustenance, but also of being provided with what we spiritually need, not the fulfilment of our wants. You will learn the difference between true 'need' and 'want'.

Then he proceeded with each line of the 'Our Father', interpreting for my child's understanding. What I learnt from him and remember was the following. I must give respect to others, and then I will gain respect. I must be aware of the evil that surrounds us. Putting my Faith in my God above, I shall be protected. I felt his teaching was his gift to me.

He counselled me that purity and goodness were the most powerful and yet the most fragile elements of life. Evil would always seek to destroy the light of the Spirit. I must guard my precious Soul and the souls of others, and in so doing, I would serve God.

'But now little one, you must begin yet another journey. We will go with light hearts, you do understand what I say. You are filled with the Light of God. Shine forth,' he said, 'from within.' He pointed to my heart. He patted my curls and kissed me on my forehead, in benediction.

After he touched me, I felt that I would share my journey not only with my mother and Stephen, but with the Lord Himself, and our beloved departed: my father who had given his life to protect us, and now Dame Elizabeth.

Stephen gathered a few belongings and closed the door to his current life, and in so doing, joined ours.

'We shall be off, Marie and Catharine, to walk in the wilderness, follow the rivers, sail on barges, being always wary of the beaten path. We will enter the monasteries for shelter before nightfall, as they will accommodate travellers. We will be brave on our journey. We shall pray together every day.'

==================

We three set out in our pilgrims' clothing. We were blessed with the clement weather of the south of France, as it was springtime. It was warm and glorious, as we journeyed northwards. There were new leaves on the trees, there were blossoms on the fruit trees, and flowers blooming everywhere. Nature was alive; colours were ablaze. At moments of respite, we would pick various flowers. My mother told me that I should always carry a small bunch; she selected the right ones for me, very carefully. My little bunch which I carried in my basket, always included plants that could heal and plants that could soothe. My mother always carried a tiny mortar and pestle so that she could crush materials into ointments and pastes, always at the ready for emergencies. I was still fearful on this journey, not knowing whether we were running away from Montpelier, departing because our Mother Elizabeth had departed this life, or perhaps running to a new life, a life she had specified for us. I wondered whether she had counted on our having the companionship of Stephen. I remember how I missed my playmates, and especially Mew-Mew and all her kittens. I missed the early morning routine, the way in which each day was governed by the bells, the hearty, yet simple meal that preceded each bedtime. But my mother and Stephen gave me comfort. It was lovely to have another hand to hold; sometimes we walked abreast, all three of us, always with me in the middle.

I hadn't thought about it much, until now, but upon reflection I must say that my mother carried with her a special aura. Her person exuded energy, yet brought a feeling of peace to all around her. She was like a magnet, always at the centre of need. Whenever we reached a hospice, it was she who was at the forefront. She would see to all of the arrangements, and comfort any at the hospice who were unwell. She insisted on giving back to the hospices that gave us shelter; that is why we were so often detained longer than the customary three days. We were often invited to stay on, but Stephen reminded us that we were on our way to Poissy, as Dame Elizabeth had directed.

How long the first part of our journey took, I cannot say.

My days were counted by the days of the Saints and by the religious calendar. Actually, it was my mother's device: we named the Saints alphabetically and called the days after them. We started with Saint Augustine, then Bartholomew, then Catherine. We got as far as Saint Peter, and then started over. My recollection is that we went through this list twice, which I guess means that we passed about thirty days travelling.

I knew about the alphabet as my mother had taught me using the names of flowers. She would write the letter and put the appropriate name of a flower, or a fruit, or a feeling beside it. A was for *'amour'*, B for 'beauty', C for 'celestial', D for 'demon', E for 'ecstasy', F for 'France'. I remember these yet. I began to learn what spelling was, from these exercises. I remembered how Pierre de Mirepoix had first introduced the idea of spelling into my experience. Stephen was there to teach me more spelling.

During our travels we were able to stop at various inns or hostelries joined to cathedrals. We would stay for two or three days. We were always offered wine and food, including soup usually made of cabbage, peas and beans, and occasionally stews of poultry, lamb, mutton or game. Coarse bread was always on offer. In summer fresh fruits and vegetables were provided; a treat of dried fruit cured with honey was typically available. We were happy with this hospitality, but the sleeping arrangements were not always good: I was very uncomfortable when the three of us had to share a bed with other travellers.

We were escorted from time to time through the more dangerous areas, otherwise our path was marked out for us by monks or by the proprietor of the inn. We were directed to the next monastery or hostelry that would welcome us. The precept was that strangers would be welcomed, just as Christ had commanded, when he said, "I was a Stranger, and you took me in." The first important town we reached was Avignon.

At Avignon we boarded a barge, going north against the flow of the river Rhone. Because the cargo had been unloaded at the southernmost point, the barge was occupied only by the bargeman and his small crew. I think that he was pleased to have our company, and I do not think that he charged us very much for the journey; after all, we didn't look like we had the where-with-all to pay. I liked watching the changing scenery as we travelled. We never lost the wonder of Spring as we went northwards; it was as if we were telling the blossoms to open as we reached them.

We disembarked at Lyon and walked for a bit. I was at first happy to be on solid ground again, although it didn't take long for me to be tired. When I was truly exhausted, we found ourselves at the gates of a large, well-managed farm. It turned out that the farmer had just died and his widow was alone. She was called Collette du Champ and offered us cosy beds of straw, and bread still warm from the oven. She noticed how tired I was and invited us to stay with her. My mother agreed that we would stay for a few days, in exchange for our help with the widow's daily chores. The widow was delighted and said that we could stay as long as we wanted. I would have embraced this choice, fresh air, wonderful food: fresh milk and fresh eggs every day. I loved being with the animals again: there were cows, pigs, sheep, chickens; I even found kittens in the barn.

My mother was aware also that Stephen was becoming ill, a fact not evident to me at that moment. This was further motivation for her to agree to stay longer with the generous widow. Stephen took a turn for the worse; it was consumption. My mother was deeply troubled; she was accustomed to caring for others, but not for those whom she truly loved. Her elixirs had no effect. The kind widow tried to help, she prepared fresh soups and breads to strengthen him, also without any effect.

Stephen's breath was failing, he was spitting blood. I saw my mother kneeling beside him by candlelight. Their dark shadows added power to the moment. She held his hand tightly in hers; they prayed together, a prayer that I had not heard before. He sat up, using all his strength. She arose, and he clasped my mother around her waist. He lay his head against her bosom, to support himself. He murmured, 'I love you; I will never leave you, I will always be with you, wherever you go. Now let us finish the Consolamentum so that I may depart this life as a *Parfait*, with you in my heart and God in my Spirit.' Stephen blessed my mother and she blessed him. He kissed her his farewell. She kissed him. His eyes closed. My mother sobbed in sorrow. I realised that I had witnessed a marriage made in heaven; my mother was again a widow.

I was so sad. I had lost my own father four years ago. I had just got used to having Stephen loving my mother and kindly caring for me. We were a real family. How much grief could I carry? My list of departed dear ones was increasing, and I did not like it.

Collette du Champ allowed us to bury Stephen just near her own beloved husband. My mother and Collette were new widows; they prayed together at the gravesite. I prayed too; my tears could not bring Stephen back.

Some time passed; Collette wanted us to stay permanently with her. She had no family and would have gladly willed her properties to us. But my mother declined. The missive we carried weighed heavily on her heart. She was obliged to deliver it.

She was intent on completing our journey. So we departed at dawn, having made a good friend of the kind Collette. We left a small purse of gold coins and a posy of fresh sweet-smelling flowers on her pillow. We were grateful that she would continue to look after Stephen's grave. We wondered afterwards how the widow reacted when she found our offering. We blessed Dame Elizabeth for making this repayment possible.

As we walked away, now alone, we passed through busy market towns, always first seeking a hostel, and then seeking some work. I noticed the changes in beds as we moved north, the blankets were thicker and the pillows softer. We carried our own muslin sheets to protect us from diseased and dirty bodies who might have lain on the beds. My mother was very hygienic for our time; she even carried our own small chamber pot with her, not wanting to contract disease from the dirty pots typically available.

So we continued, it did not take very long to reach the point just beyond Lyon where we were able to board another barge to take us north to Chalon-sur-Saône. Like north-going barges on the Rhone, this barge was not heavily laden, and there was no difficulty in getting passage. When we arrived at Chalon-sur-Saône we had another saint-list worth of walking to do (about a fortnight) before we found the very beginning of the Seine. We knew that the Seine would take us towards Paris, and to Poissy, where we could deliver Dame Elizabeth's missive. We wondered what Poissy might hold for us.

By the time we boarded our final barge, on the Seine, it was already summer. The Seine carried us slowly at first, but soon at a heady speed, as we were flowing in the direction the river went, not opposite as had been the case on the Rhone and on the Saône. The scow stopped along the riverbank from time to time, to take on provisions and passengers, as well as goods to be traded at the market in Paris. I enjoyed watching all this activity. I felt excited. Goods in all shapes and sizes arrived on board. The gruff words were different to the ones I knew; the speaking sounds were so different that I could hardly understand anything. My mother managed, just.

The closer we got to our destination, the more we heard about preparations for the coronation of Queen Isabeau, that was due to occur very soon in Paris. This was the first time I heard the name of our Queen, and my curiosity was aroused.

Chapter III

Dame Marie at Poissy

-1389 -

Ever this day (night)
Be at my side
To light and guard,
Rule and guide.

We told the bargeman that we had been directed to bring a message to Poissy, and asked him to advise us when to disembark. He put us off on the south bank of the Seine, and told us to enquire at the Church for directions. We did.

We saw first the open fields, and then there was an impressive stone wall, beyond which we knew lay Poissy. We arrived at the gate of this Dominican convent, which Dame Elizabeth had told us was officially known as the convent of St Louis. We were allowed in by a wise old nun, who spent her days there determining who was worthy to enter.

Inside the wall, our eyes took in the order and beauty in the vast expanse of the convent. It was magnificent! There were splendid buildings; it was truly paradise on earth that unfolded before us as we entered this sanctuary. There was an orchard with hundreds of fruit trees, there was a walled park where animals like deer, hare, rabbit, and wild goat roamed free. There were ponds stocked with fish. There were ducks and geese that swam on the river. It was a self-sufficient estate, a well-endowed community unto itself. We saw that there was a large farm which served the convent, from within its own walls. There was a separate section to house the men who were required to help with the heavy labour.

We were momentarily stunned into silence by this first impression of the place.

But we remembered that we were carrying our letter from Dame Elizabeth. So we requested a meeting with the Prioress, Dame Marie (de Bourbon), who was herself a Royal Princess, sister-in-law of Charles V, and the aunt of our present king. The nun who gave us entry directed us to the hospice for travellers, and told us to wash away the dust of travel to make ourselves ready to be received by Dame Marie. We were given food and rest and fresh clothing. I was particularly impressed by the beds which we were given to use, as I had taken to noticing beds everywhere. My mother's bed was webbed at the bottom, with a mattress of feathers on it, and under her bed was a cot on wheels, just for me, my own bed! There were sheets and blankets, which were cleaner than any we had seen on our journey.

When we were rested, we were summoned to Dame Marie.

We entered the parlour, which was the room where visitors were received. It was beautifully furnished. These surroundings were more like a royal court than a nunnery. After we curtseyed deeply, Dame Marie greeted us warmly and with compassion, seeing the fatigue in our faces, which she seemed to notice without directly looking. Her face was surrounded by a tight white bonnet, a black veil covered her hair and her shoulders. Her oval face was serene, soft, and smooth. She was so beautiful to my eyes, that I could only imagine that the Virgin Mary, Mother of Christ, was embodied in her. She displayed no emotion. Her words were calming and quiet.

She asked us to sit beside her, and folded her hands on her

lap. My mother took a seat, but I crouched at Dame Marie's feet, as I had done in the presence of Dame Elizabeth. I felt immediately warm towards her, but my mother exercised more caution, knowing in advance that she was not of the Cathar faith. My mother was indeed more consciously respectful, because she was aware that Dame Marie was of royal blood.

My mother handed her Dame Elizabeth's letter. Whilst she was reading, we looked around the room. I noticed the tapestries, the jewelled cross, various paintings of our King Charles V, where the artist had captured a sense of wisdom in his likeness. There was also a portrait of King Charles V with Queen Jeanne of Bourbon, Dame Marie's sister. There was one portrait of Charles VI showing his handsome and sensitive features. I really felt that I was in the presence of the good and the great.

I wondered about Dame Marie and about everything around us. Had she been in the nunnery since the age of five? Had she made this choice herself? Was she simply a widow who had chosen to live out her years in peace and contemplation? She was so beautiful that I could imagine that there would have been many royal suitors seeking her hand. Was my mother intending to join this Dominican order as a working nun? What did Dame Elizabeth's missive suggest that my mother should do? Should she join this convent as a healer and an herb gardener? And what was to become of me? Was I holy enough and inspired enough to follow in such footsteps?

Dame Marie looked up after she finished reading the letter. She directed her first words to me. She said, 'Catharine, I would like to know you better. Dame Elizabeth has written about you in glowing terms. She loved you very much. I wonder if you might like to accompany me on some of my visits within these walls to the farms and orchards and gardens. I would love to teach you about this sanctuary.'

I curtseyed again and began to twirl about, my spirit delighted by this turn of events.

Then Dame Marie turned to my mother. 'Marie, we do need you here. Healing is always required. Dame Elizabeth recommends you highly, and has mentioned many of the minor miracles you have performed by the grace of God, with your skills. I receive you with open arms. Now I will have you shown to your permanent quarters; I will for the moment, allow your daughter to stay with you. We shall make the appropriate arrangements for Catharine later on.'

But then the bells rang, interrupting our conversation. I was delighted to be summoned again by the Angelus. Life would again be ordered. We followed Dame Marie to the chapel, resuming the practical matters afterwards.

The service in the chapel was more elegant than any I had experienced before. I relished the singing and was so happy to say my prayers aloud. We blessed our Pope Clement VII, who was seated at Avignon. There was some reference to the Great Schism, about which everyone spoke in hushed tones, praying for the defeat of the Papacy in Rome. I didn't understand any of this, I just wanted the clarity of knowing that our pope was guiding us.

Once evening benediction was over, we were escorted to our new quarters, which consisted of a large chamber, with beds arranged the same way as we had earlier experienced. This time we did not need to use our travelling sheets because the sheets were clean and smelled of lavender.

We left our few belongings in our quarters, and went immediately to the refectory where our evening meal was served. We met some of the nuns, who smiled their greeting and their welcome to us. We said grace aloud, one of the nuns read a passage from the Bible, whilst we ate. We had a light meal of bread, cheese, and fresh fruit. We took our leave after we had eaten.

With Dame Marie's permission, we wandered in the fragrant gardens. The blend of perfumes: lavender with rose, mint with rosemary and thyme, geranium with linden blossoms; they all combined to bring me the memory of our home in Carcassone. I felt safe and happy.

We were drawn, of course, to the herb garden and were totally enchanted with the abundance and variety of plants and herbs growing there. It was as if my mother had been given the means to heal the ills of all mankind. She hugged me, with great excitement. 'Catharine, you now see, just before your eyes, everything in one place, as we have never seen it before.' She took my hands in hers, and in jubilant thanks, we repeated the Pater Noster nine times. She felt secure in being able to practice her healing art here, without threat or scrutiny. We still thought of Dame Elizabeth who had sent us; she must have foreseen that the position at Poissy to look after the herb garden would require my mother. As it happened, the old mistress of the garden had recently departed this life. We prayed for her soul, and gave her thanks for her absence at our critical time. We also prayed for the souls of my father and of Stephen; we felt their protection around us. We picked a few heads of lavender and pressed them between our palms, and then inhaled the perfume which revived our spirits after our turmoil and travel.

We returned to our quarters by candlelight. My mother took out her small vessel of distilled rosewater. She dabbed our faces and bodies with a small flannel which she soaked in it, to cool us. We lay peacefully on our beds, and dreamt of the many happy tomorrows we would enjoy at this convent.

====================

BOOK II

Christine de Pisan:

Her own story and Her view of the Royals

Chapter IV

Christine de Pisan

from 1368 -

*'Blessed is the man that walketh not in the counsel of
the ungodly
Nor standeth in the way of sinners
Nor sitteth in the seat of the scornful.
But his delight is in the law of the Lord
And in his law doth he meditate day and night.
And he shall be like a tree planted by the rivers of water
That bringeth forth his fruit in his season;
His leaf also shall not wither
And whatsoever he doeth shall prosper.'* [3]

I, Christine was a child of four, when something quite extraordinary happened. Was it an upset, or was it a delight? My father, Tommaso di Benvenuto da Pisano, was absent, as he was at the Court of Charles V, le Sage, of France.

My father had accepted the King's invitation to a position at his Court as his Astrologer and Physician in 1364, which was the year I was born. He had promised my mother that he would only be absent for a year, during which time, my mother was charged with looking after all of the family properties in

---

[3] Psalm 1

Bologna. We moved to Bologna then; naturally, I had no recollection of Venice, the city where I was born.

After the first year, my father was enticed to remain, as he had made himself indispensable to the King, who offered him a wonderful reward for staying, including a home, properties, and income, as well as the relocation of my mother and me to join him. My father was still hopeful that he could return to Venice, in fact that we could all be reunited there. Therefore he delayed his decision for another two years.

Finally, when I was four, a letter was delivered to my mother which summoned us to Paris. We were to live at the Court of the King. As it was already early autumn, we were told to leave in all haste. My mother thought this a disruptive upheaval, coming only three years after the move from Venice to Bologna. Closing up the family home was no easy task. But our real fear was the foreboding venture across the Alps.

We packed our most important possessions, and bade farewell to our closest friends and family. My father had organised that we travel with a group of trusted merchants, who were delivering goods from the Near East. We dressed in comfortable layers against the expected cold of the journey. I wore a plain linen tunic underneath. My mother had sewn precious jewels and gold coins into the hem of this undergarment. Over this tunic, I wore a dark brown shift of light weight wool. We both wore '*bourrelets*' (padded circlet hats) on their heads. We children wore them to protect us in the event of a fall, but my mother wore hers to augment the base of her elegant head-dress. My mother had also sewn valuables which my father had entrusted to her care, into our *bourrelets*. I bore some of the jewels on my body, in addition to the ones sewn into my hems. (I really didn't care for these weighty responsibilities.) My mother had sewn a great many more into the hems of her heavy skirts. We wore soft handmade leather ankle boots, which were comfortable and warm. We had blankets of sheepskin, and hooded capes – mine was lined in beaver, whilst my mother's was lined with sable. I liked the feel of these soft furry garments.

My mother could not hide her fear. Great was her anxiety, protecting me on this journey. Before we departed, she spent many hours at the church where her Will and Testament were prepared. Here many prayers were said for our safety and psalms were sung to bless us. She gave money for the poor of our area and for the servants we left behind. She was given letters of introduction from the Church, and also many from her friends, to help us on our way.

So we were off, in a grand caravan, seated in a covered cart, drawn by mules. The canvas cover was elaborately decorated and fitted over an arched frame. We had been advised to use mules, as horses would require frequent changing on a journey as long as ours. Other mules carried our supplies and the merchandise being transported for trade in Paris. It seemed a great adventure when we departed, accompanied by the colourful protective guards.

I recall the day of our departure: autumn was trying to take over the scene. The leaves were golden and red, demonstrating that they had captured the sun, seeking to hold it just a bit longer. The vines in our area had been picked; the scent of fermenting grapes permeated the air. I had just run through these vines yesterday picking off remaining sweet grapes to taste. We had sunshine on the morning we left, sunshine that had just arrived following the strong winds and rain that had caused the early picking, and cooled and dampened the air. My senses responded to this atmosphere, and I felt sadness in leaving, although my excitement to encounter the unknown, including reunion with my father, overtook my feeling of regret in departing the familiar.

As a child, I was soon uncomfortable. I was accustomed to running and playing out of doors, not sitting for hours on end, jostled by the uneven motion of the wheels on the bumpy trails. I tried to amuse myself by looking at the different world, the varying landscapes that presented themselves as we travelled. We passed the harvested fields and more grapeless vines. We were caught by gusty winds; coloured falling leaves decorated our path. We had our own servants with us, who were equally uneasy in this undertaking of the unknown.

Our cart was drawn in a north-westerly direction, over relatively flat ground towards Milano. Our mules were sure-footed over the narrow trails.

The look-out scout, with his fleet-footed horse preceded us on our route. When he had ascertained that the path was safe, he returned and directed Angelo, who was our guide from Bologna, who had agreed to accompany us until we reached the Alps. We travelled about fifteen to twenty miles a day, making camp in the evening. Then my mother and I would sleep in our cart because we didn't want to lie on the hard, cold ground. I clung to my mother, as the night noises sounded threatening to me. I always felt reassured when the night watchman of our party would circle the camp and shout that all was well.

It was always a relief to reach a monastery. I remember once that when my mother presented her letter of introduction, all of the caravan were invited to lodge there. We were announced, and the abbot and brothers greeted us in complete fulfilment of their loving Christian duty. We knew that we were truly blessed when we had been kissed by the abbot. Then the abbot and monks washed the feet of our scout, our guards and servants, the ultimate expression of Christian love. We and the merchants, who accompanied us, were offered a bath to be thoroughly refreshed. After we had cleaned our bodies, we were summoned to the refectory. The hall was warmed by the crackling blaze within the large stone fireplace. A hearty meal of pasta and soup, accompanied by crusty bread with olive oil, cold meats, and cheese, was provided. Wine from the monastery's own vineyard was served. We were given a large room to share just off the dining room; there was a private latrine just outside. The bed was large and comfortable. We rested for several days.

Our travel pattern was like that, from camp to monastery to inn. I remember the feeling, the constant motion and then the stopping, but the details all blend together.

After about a fortnight, we neared Milano. There we were received with great warmth by the prominent Visconti family, to whom we had been referred by King Charles V. His sister Isabelle was married into this family. The elegant Isabelle welcomed us and saw to all our needs. We were surrounded by luxury: I remember the soft beds covered by sheets of silk. I really would have liked to stay there. But my mother was impatient to rejoin my father, even though the path to reach him was long. I had no real memory of my father, as I was only one when he had been invited to France. I remembered that, when I was alone with my mother in our bedchamber there, she whispered to me that my father must indeed be well-loved by his majesty Charles le Sage, to extend such gracious support to us on our journey.

We were advised to travel to Aosta, in the southern alpine area. There we left our mules and carts, ready for the returning merchants to use. We were given guards and guides who would help us to get across the Alps.

We arrived in mid-October and collected supplies and litters. At the hostelry, the Visconti guards from Milano selected a whole team of porters from the local area. The porters were excellent mountaineers who knew the details of our intended path. Because the patron for our journey was the King himself, they were well compensated.

It was very early in the morning when we departed for our climb over the mountains. My mother and I, and others who were unused to negotiating these heights, were placed on litters and carried. The uneven terrain and altitude would wreak havoc on us women of gentle birth, unaccustomed to the rigors of arduous life. We could see snow on the distant and imposing peaks, which we knew we would soon encounter. Part of me was thrilled and part of me was scared. We saw sheep and goats returning to the lower plains from their summer pastures in the mountains. We heard the clanging bells that announced their presence to all, the shepherds followed quickly behind, nearly as nimble as their flocks. The sights around us were totally new to me. I felt close to God in the mountain heights, and light-headed so near to the sky's blue canopy.

As a child it was just an adventure. I could not feel the fear and strain that my elders felt, on this hazardous journey. At moments I wished I was a bird, so that I wouldn't feel the rocking from side to side, forwards and backwards, as I was carried. I thought that the journey would be much faster as well, to glide on wing over the mountainside. But we couldn't escape the jostling. Our porters would sing, chanting the praises of the angels and saints, asking them to guide their feet securely on these treacherous paths. (Our lives were truly in their hands.)

By nightfall we arrived in a monastery, all alone amongst the peaks. We were given shelter and frugal fare. I was exhausted from this first day's alpine travel, but I did not complain. I could not dare to; the litter-bearers must have been beyond exhaustion. In the mountain air, we slept deeply, although I was still struggling to breathe it.

The next day, our porters took up their burden again. We followed the contour of the paths that the guides had chosen for us. There was now a little snow on the mountains, and we wondered how the porters managed to find the precise route that took us safely forward. The weather varied: at one moment there was light, and the next minute there were snowy clouds and blustery winds. My mother told me that we had our guardian angels watching over us. My impatience, however, was growing. It felt as though it was taking forever. My mother and I both wanted to see my father. Our longing to see him replaced the fear we had begun to feel as we were proceeding.

A day or so later, we could see that we were descending the mountains. We saw the start of the River Rhone at the foot. There were boatmen waiting for us there. We were so excited to see them. I was quite ready to continue, but the decision was taken that we rest, so we took lodging at a small inn. Eventually we embarked on the waiting boat, following the Rhone on its path to Lake Geneva, and westward from there. Our guards and guides from the Visconti family stayed with us, and negotiated for local support as we journeyed.

I cannot recall all the details of this expedition. It seemed endless. We had seen so many changes in scenery and experienced so many changes in fare, that I was feeling quite confused by then. The language around us had changed as well. I was grateful for the now familiar staff, that surrounded us from Milano, because I could still ask them questions and understand their answers.

On a cold day in December, we arrived, with our retinue, by barge on the Seine, at the Palais du Louvre. We were welcomed, not only by my father, but also by the King. The King was so handsome, he looked like a god to me. He had an air of calm and his voice was at a perfect timbre. I could not understand him, but I liked the sound of his voice.

We were richly but differently attired in our Lombard fashion, lavishly embroidered with golden threads and precious stones. As it was so cold, we were wrapped in furs.

The warmth of the reception combated the frost. I felt intimidated but exalted at being launched into the most sumptuous court in the whole world. (My father whispered all truths to me when he picked me up into his arms, and kissed me. In a hushed voice, he also told me that I should express my happiness for being with my father, and also for being in the home of His Most Handsome and Wise King, to His Majesty.) I prepared my little speech in Italian. The king was astonished to hear my words, and I believe that he understood me. My mother was silent and shy in my father's presence; she was also uncomfortable in the presence of the King. I felt that my father was respected for his intelligence in the areas of astronomy and foreign affairs, his language skills, but also as physician to the King.

After this initial encounter, my father took us to our quarters in the palace. We moved after some time to a private palace in the St-Paul district. It seemed that my father could afford anything we wanted, and he spoilt me terribly.

I had a charmed childhood, on the banks of the Seine, without grief or sorrow. This beginning gave me great confidence which I carried into my later life.

If there is anything that I can say that was wrong with my education, it was the restrictions that my mother sought to place on me. Her view was that I should learn the female crafts: embroidery, sewing, and beautiful singing. I found these activities to be a waste of time, and gravitated towards discussions with my father.

My father and I shared interests in the universe: sciences, mathematics, literature and law. I was immersed in philosophy and thoughts. Socrates, Plato, Aristotle: I said their names, letting the sounds roll round my mouth like a spell or a prayer. These men became my friends of the mind. I learnt about the Roman strengths in the stories of the Caesars, including their military prowess and their legions of invasions which brought order of Law to the peoples they conquered. Pythagoras featured in my understanding of distance and calculations. The Hippocratic code was conveyed to me; I, like my father, was fascinated with the principles of healing. The sun, the moon and their companions, the stars, fascinated me. The hidden, but known constellations that gave the signs of the Zodiac, ruled our lives from the moment of birth. I felt that understanding the celestial movements of these spheres, was the path on which my soul could approach God. Acquiring that knowledge increased my appreciation for the heavens above and my existence below.

Instead of staying close to my mother, who was in the full bloom of producing my two younger brothers Aginolfo and Paolo, one right after the other, I frequently escaped into my father's study. He allowed me to read his beautiful manuscripts. They were wonderful, bound in leather with ornamentation in gold. My fingers thrilled to the touch of these books; the musty scent of the worn parchment pages made me feel kinship with the learned who had touched them before. I was dazzled by the illustrations, brilliantly coloured, with the blue of lapis, the red of ruby and the green of crushed malachite. I traced the letters with my fingers, feeling the textures of ink and colour. The experience was beyond the visual, the tactile aspect enticed me to learn to read the different styles of the various scribes and understand their artistic perseverance.

I was also allowed access to the king's library. Gilles Malet, the librarian, enjoyed my company because of my serious interest in learning. He placed the precious books on the massive slanted stands for me to read. He moved the bench closer, so that I could stand on it, as I was not as tall as the monks and professors who used the library. I read Aesops fables, various books of poetry, Bible stories, and stories of animals, all with wonderful illustrations. When I think back on those moments, I know that they opened the door to my destiny.

My father had for a long time desperately wanted sons. I am afraid that he was somewhat disappointed after they arrived, however. Despite his extreme efforts to incite in them the love of learning, their interest was limited. He was, in the end, grateful to have me to share his pursuit of knowledge. I was thankful for this natural selection. I was not shunted aside as so many young girls were.

My life and my education, including my reluctant acquisition of those mundane "female" skills, continued in this way, until I reached the age of about thirteen years. By then, I could read in other languages, including ancient Greek and Hebrew, the sounds of which were mysterious and exotic, the letters strangely shaped like squares and flowers. I was skilled enough socially, to accompany my father at court, and attend the most splendid receptions when our King entertained foreign royals. My mother quickly lost interest in these occasions; but the King insisted on my presence. I was honoured by these opportunities and wrote an account of them, as a chronicler. It was a deep thinking, strange world for a young girl, but I had grown to thrive in it.

At this time, there was a change in my life. I became aware of the presence of the King's young notary, a member of the chancellery. He caused such an excitement within me, even if I just passed him in the corridor: the air seemed to hum around him. My father noticed my transformation: I was suddenly breathless and blushing. He asked me what preoccupied me. I described this young man to my father, who recognised him from my description.

My father quietly thought about my future, and considered the kind of husband I should have. He thought that my attraction to this young notary might be just the right match.

He was Etienne de Castel. He was ten years older than me, indeed eligible for courtship. I was, however, a bit young. But, I did have presence and education, and had always been unusually evolved. My father mentioned this possibility to the King and an official courtship was arranged.

I stole furtive glances in his direction, and was overwhelmed that Etienne was so handsome. He carried himself with grace and confidence. He was trusted by the King, and deemed to have a good future before him. But most important to me, were his kindness, his affection, his thoughtfulness and his intelligence. We both enjoyed life at Court, and he was impressed with, not threatened by, my learning. It was with great joy that we were betrothed with the King's blessing.

In the early spring of 1379, we were married. King Charles V offered the wedding celebration as a gift to my father. He gave us a dowry, in addition to that which my father provided. My only sadness at this event was the fact that our beloved King was suffering from ill health. My father had been unable to diagnose his complaint, and hence the ailment went untreated. I felt that he was really suffering from a broken heart, after his wife Queen Jeanne had departed this life two years before. I had seen her passing take its toll on him.

Our wedding was a spectacular affair. My father and Etienne both looked handsome. My mother and my brothers were dressed in Lombard style finery, sewn for them here in Paris.

I felt so blessed, in having found Etienne. 'It seemed to me that he had no equal in all the world, for my dearest wish could not have been for a person more wise, prudent, handsome, kind or better than him in any way.... We had so arranged our love and our two hearts that we had just one single entire will, whether in joy or sorrow, closer than brothers or sisters. His company was so pleasing to me that when he was near me there wasn't a woman alive more completely satisfied with every blessing. In every way within his power, with all sorts of pleasing trifles, comforts and delicacies, he made life easier for me.[4]

---

[4] The Path of Long Study, lines 78-97, by Christine de Pisan

Chapter V

Charles V

-- from 1364 -

'Hear this, all ye people;
Give ear, all ye inhabitants of the world:
Both low and high, rich and poor, together,
My mouth shall speak of wisdom;
And the meditation of my heart shall be of
understanding....'[5]

I, Christine, was commissioned by Philippe le Hardi[6], duc de Bourgogne, in 1404, to write a biography of Charles V. I was allowed to read the Wise King's own manuscripts and the time-table of his daily life, as a part of my research. My childhood memories about him were overwhelmingly evoked. Bureau de la Rivière[7] granted me interviews, so his memories are blended with mine.

How I got to this point, will be described later. But I will now tell the story of our beloved and wise King, who influenced me profoundly.

---

[5] Psalm 49
[6] Philippe the Bold
[7] Chamberlain and advisor to King Charles V; belonged to the trusted group known as the Marmosets

He was not a handsome man, he was thin and frail in appearance. His nose was long and narrow, his mouth like a slit, but his eyes sparkled, revealing his great intelligence and sensitivity. He had an inner strength that came to the fore in adversity. It allowed him to deal with difficulties in an adroit fashion.

He became the king in 1364, upon the death of his father Jean II, after having been Regent since 1356 when Jean was captured at Poitiers by the English. It was an ill conceived battle, on the part of the French. In fact, Jean was arrogantly foolish in taking on the superiority of the well equipped and annoying English. Charles was deeply affected by this turn of events; he took this experience to heart and allowed it to inspire him to plan his future. He decided that under his regency, and under his reign, his first alternative would be to negotiate. In addition he would select the best military commander to do his fighting and carefully plan the strategies for war. For himself, he reserved the space to rule majestically.

Unfortunately it took until his actual reign for Charles to fully implement this strategy. In 1356, he was only the Dauphin. He had to exert humility, for the time being, to the tradesmen, whose resources he required to negotiate his father's freedom. It took him some time to achieve his father's release. It was not until the Treaty of Brétigny was signed in May 1360, and a large ransom promised, that Jean was returned to France.

The ransom remained unpaid for quite some time. Raising the money was a difficult task, a task which Charles sought to avoid. In 1364, by which time Jean was frustrated that the honour of this promise had not yet been settled, Jean determined officially to return to England, again as hostage, to show his good faith. In truth he was returning to the company of his beautiful young English Countess (purported to be the Countess of Salisbury), who had become his mistress during his imprisonment before. Jean was greeted in London by Edward III and lavishly entertained before returning to a cosy and comfortable captivity, where several months later he fell ill of a mysterious ailment and died. He was given the most splendid funeral with songs and blazing candles at St Paul's Cathedral. His body was placed in a beautiful coffin and returned to France by sea.

Charles the Dauphin had meanwhile been preparing for his eventual role in some ways; he married Jeanne de Bourbon in 1350. She was gentle and kind and seduced him with great finesse.

But he became bored. He developed other relationships. There were at least two notable mistresses, who bore him illegitimate children.

By contrast, when he became king, Charles became truly pious, living by a strict religious time table. He awoke at a very early hour, made the sign of the cross and prayed, and offered his day to God. Once he had completed his morning ablutions and was dressed, he was presented with his breviary. He prayed with his chaplain and attended High Mass in his private chapel. He then attended Low Mass in his private oratory, where hymns were sung. The harmonious melodies gave him great joy at the opening of his day.

When his religious rituals were completed, he went directly to his court. Frequently he allowed all ranks of his subjects to be included in his audience: men and women, old and young, maidens and widows. On specific days he presided over matters of State.

He was a regal king, fully conscious of the importance of the crown of France and his role to protect it.

At midday, that is about ten o'clock in the morning, he dined, whilst listening to his minstrels playing tunes to uplift his soul. After his repast, he received foreign dignitaries, aristocrats, and knights who brought their matters before him. They told him their tales of bravery, of losses, of gains, of riches, and of the poverty they had encountered, both in France and on foreign soil. It was thanks to these moments that he was able to envisage the current affairs of the times. His decisions, therefore, were based on knowledge, and his strategies for ruling were very, very wise.

After these sessions, he signed letters and documents. He gave gifts to ambassadors and despatched with them various tokens to be presented to their sovereigns. He also received gifts from the notables present.

After a few moments of rest, he would indulge in the sweet interludes that he loved the most, in the company of his wife and children. Jeanne de Bourbon was now truly his wife; as king he rediscovered her. He adored her. They held hands and prayed together. He played with his children. He was happy to be just a husband and father for a short time.

This was his typical routine.

He was careful, and disposed to astrological advice. In 1364, as we already have mentioned, he summoned my father, Thomas de Pisan to join his court. He also took counsel from Nicolas Oresme[8], who was more scientific in approach. There were also suggestions from the clerics who surrounded him. Charles found his own wisdom in the balance amongst the varied counsels.

The clear voice of common sense was the one Charles followed. His true and loyal Marmosets[9] provided an administrative system that both supported his wisdom in internal matters, and helped to ease the path of negotiation with his enemies. It was due to these diplomatic discussions that he was able to maintain relative peace during his reign.

In addition to ruling during these challenging times, Charles did encounter some difficulties with the Queen. She was afflicted with a touch of madness in 1373, and lost much of her memory. Charles in his piety prayed for her; he took himself on several pilgrimages for her, and as if by miracle, she slowly regained her sanity and memories. She bore him five daughters and two sons. These daughters died, but the sons survived. Then in 1377, she was again in pains of childbirth. Death overcame her as she gave life to her only surviving

---

[8] learned counsellor to King Charles V, specialised in mathematics, astronomy, and economics; sceptical about the preaching of the clergy at the time; opponent to Thomas de Pisan.

[9] bourgeois-born councillors

daughter Catherine.

Charles suddenly felt his mortality intensely. He had lost his beloved wife. He returned to his private chapel to mourn her. He wept.

He tried to reign as before, but found himself incapable of retrieving his former strength. He was so alone, without his Jeanne. His grief continued, and did not abate in intensity.

Three years later, on the 13th July, his chief military advisor, Bertrand du Guesclin died. Charles was again devastated, and very alone. He felt it was all too much to endure. He was afflicted with constant pain, both physical and mental, and continued to weaken daily. On the 21st August 1380 he was so ill that he was taken to his mansion at Beauté where he stayed alone seeking solace. This beautiful home was located in a park, surrounded by an ivy-covered wall. It had often given him respite and peace in the past.

His two sons Charles and Louis were obliged to stay in Melun at this time, as there was a very serious epidemic raging in Paris and its environs.

All through the night of the 13th September, until Friday the 14th September, the king suffered a cruel and gripping heart attack. In the morning he called his confessor, confessed his sins, and heard Mass. He asked for Holy Communion, but could hardly manage to swallow the host. His pain continued and increased. He then developed a very high fever, and began to ramble deliriously. This episode continued for some time. He then became calm, exhausted by the torture of the preceding period.

On Sunday, the 16th September, he was suddenly searching for breath, and gestured that he desired to be moved to his *chaise-longue*. He summoned his favourite advisors and his son Charles.

His own mortality was not foremost in his mind, even at this time. His greatest worry was the Schism[10]. He strongly believed that Clement VII, the French Pope[11], was the right shepherd

---

[10] From 1378 there was a Pope in Rome and another Pope in Avignon.
[11] in Avignon

for the Church. He meant that everyone who followed the Faith should adhere to this position. He felt this sincerely, without national bias.

He renounced all the taxes which had caused severe burdens on his people.

At midday, Charles half stood up. The priests had arrived, and brought with them their Holy Oils. Charles received the Sacrament of Extreme Unction. At that moment all the clergy and the people who surrounded the king, moved to the far end of the room and began weeping. The dying king begged forgiveness of all those whom he might have hurt during his life. He blessed his beloved son Charles, aged 12, and told him that he would soon be charged with ruling this most beautiful country. Charles V had already taken the precaution of enacting a special ruling, by which young Charles would reach majority and thereby the right to rule as king, at the age of 14 years. The nation's torments would cease in peace, the dying king advised, providing the young king took a compassionate and reasonable approach to his reign. The king died in the arms of Bureau de la Rivière, his most wise and trusted courtier, during the reading of Christ's Passion by the officiating clergy.

Ten days later, Charles' body was taken to St Denis to lie in state, for burial in the presence of his tearful countrymen and his greedy brothers.

======================

The funeral was a resplendent event. The basilica at St Denis was decked with flowers; the attendance was overwhelming for the beloved King. The child king Charles VI stood resolutely with his brother Louis, doing his utmost to appear dignified whilst on the verge of tears. I and my husband Etienne de Castel felt a great emptiness within, knowing that the loss of our wise king would cause our lives to change dramatically. But we put on a brave demeanour, and stopped to speak with the young Royals. I reminded Charles and Louis that I had revered their father since I was a child. I promised Charles that Etienne and I would be forever loyal to him; I cautioned him to take care, as undoubtedly many would wish to get into his good favour, for their own interests. He must soon reign over France, and good counsel would be required.

======================

Unfortunately the legacy that the dead king had wanted for his country did not come to pass. The country was beset by revolts of the working classes and the poor, as the promised tax repeals were delayed, and eventually annulled, and instead increased. Government was taken over by the brothers of Charles V.

The elder brother, known as Louis I, duc d'Anjou, was energetic, tenacious, and devoured by ambition. After having endured being held hostage by the English in his father's place some years before, he distinguished himself first by escaping, then, by taking on the English in Guyenne with great bravado. He had certain undeniable qualities: an imposing personality, always finding the right manipulative word at the right time. He was both regal and haughty but also courageous. He was both artistic and intellectual; he acquired some of the most exquisite volumes from his brother's splendid library. He was a sly opportunist, and without scruples where money and wealth were concerned. As the eldest surviving brother to Charles V, he was the First Regent, and used his position to drain the treasury. At the same moment he spoke soothing words to the poor of France, promising tax repeal to assuage their anger, or to turn their rage against others in power, or alternatively against the Jewish money lenders.

His ambition was clear; he wanted to be king; if not of France, then another kingdom would do. He found his opportunity, when Jeanne, the heirless Queen of Naples, invited him to become her heir, and hence the eventual King of Naples. Louis I, duc d'Anjou, had to take a great fortune with him then, as dues had to be paid to the Roman Pope for this fiefdom. He emptied the treasury to contribute to this end. It was all for naught, however, as Pope Urban VI, had already confirmed another candidate as heir to the Naples throne. The throne of Naples had become Louis' unfinished dream.

Jean, duc de Berri, was the second brother of Charles V. His only interest was to achieve his desires; he had no interest in duties. He was vain and sensual: heavily built with a large unprepossessing face. He was cunning, and surrounded himself with the most exquisite luxuries, also funded by the legacy his late brother Charles V, had unwittingly provided. He was greedy for rich foods, exotic fruits, and beautiful women, but his greatest passion was for the arts. He acquired a grand collection of ornate and bejewelled volumes for his own library. He collected jewels, paintings, tapestries, and statues. He assured his life style, by promises to those who would bribe him. Yet he was generous with his 'favourites,' with whom he indulged his passions. This generosity, and also his love of animals, were the enduring qualities which allowed his vices to be somewhat forgiven.

Philippe le Hardi, duc de Bourgogne, was the youngest brother. He had gained the appellation, 'le Hardi', at the battle of Poitiers where he had shown himself to be very courageous, at an age of barely 15 years. His weakness was his overwhelming desire for power.

Louis II of Bourbon, was the brother-in-law of Charles V. He was the least dishonest of this governing committee. His influence was weak; he was often depressed and died mad. He actually contributed very little to the ensuing reign, which had ample negative contribution from Charles VI's other uncles.

====================

As I said, when I started to tell the story of my beloved King Charles V, my purpose was just to give a summary – just so that you would understand the personalities that dominated these times. I trust that this has been accomplished.

I must also mention, in all sadness, that Philippe le Hardi died on the 25th April 1404, just before I completed the first tome of this biography on the 28th April, four months after I had started writing. Jean sans Peur[12] who succeeded him as the Duc de Bourgogne, was devastated.

Philippe le Hardi had paid me an advance for my efforts, but full payment was not forthcoming at this time.

>Christine de Pisan de Castell
>May 1404.

---

[12] Jean the Fearless

Chapter VI

Charles VI

– 1380 –

*'Save me, O God; for the waters are come in unto my soul.
I sink in deep mire, where there is no standing:
I am come into deep waters, where the floods
overflow me.'*[13]

Charles and Louis lost their mother in 1377; in 1380 they lost their father. The pressure was on the eldest of these two. Charles became king.

He was pious in his very early years, giving numerous gifts to the Church. He attained his greatest joy, as a pilgrim to Notre-Dame in Paris.

Charles was called the well-beloved; he loved to be loved. He was handsome and charming, generous and gentle. His generosity was not confined to the material; he gave easily to the needy, and also to those who were not. He was unable to refuse anyone. In all his qualities, however, there was a weakness, the weakness of heredity, caused by inbreeding. His mother was the first cousin of his father; his grandfather and his grandmother had also been first cousins.

---

[13] Psalm 69

He was given a fine upbringing: his father had proscribed him a perfect education, equipping him both intellectually and morally to take on the role of King. Amongst his tutors was Phillipe de Mézières, who was knowledgeable in the sciences, enlightened in the spiritual, and highly moral. By the age of seven, Charles had been exposed to many of the important works of literature and the sciences. He read extensively, benefiting from his father's magnificent library.

Unbeknownst to his father, he was also precociously sexual. One of the courtiers introduced him to the pleasures of the flesh at the early age of twelve, filling in an important gap in his education. When Charles V discovered this occurrence, however, the courtier was immediately banished from the Court.

Charles was neither tall, nor short. He had well-developed, sturdy limbs. He had a powerfully broad chest. He was of light complexion. His lively eyes sparkled. His nose was perfectly shaped, neither too long nor too short. But the crowning glory of his appearance was his fair, fair hair. He was truly handsome.

He was gracefully athletic. As a youth, he was ideal material for knighthood. As a warrior, he was able to use all the arms needful in battle. He was also an excellent horseman. He was brave in the face of adversity. He was often involved in tournaments, bested by few, in stark contrast with Charles V who instead engaged champions and generals to lead his battles. He was indeed the ideal prince, nearly ready to become the ideal king, even though his intellect was not at the same level as that of his father.

But he was now the King. His uncles were the ruling Regents. They conspired to relieve the treasury of its riches, whilst Charles was growing into his new role. He moved to l'Hôtel St-Pôl, to distance himself from the Court intrigues and to find personal peace.

Chapter VII

The Paris of Charles V and Charles VI

1374 -1399

'Keep not thou silence, O God:
Hold not thy peace, and be not still, O God.
For, lo thine enemies make a tumult:
And they that hate thee have lifted up the head.
They have taken crafty counsel against thy people,
And consulted against thy hidden ones.
They have said, Come, and let us cut them off from being
a nation....'[14]

These were desperate times throughout the continent of Europe; Paris was a city where the peoples' desperation demanded an eight o'clock night time curfew. The bells of Notre Dame chimed to send the people home. They lit no fires, fearful of any possible inferno that could be fuelled by the rubbish in the streets and the wooden houses. Arson was feared.

The darkened streets belonged to vagabonds and truants, thieves and murderers, kidnappers and bandits. There was no safety for anyone: whether they lived in a hovel or a palace, no one was without fear. Criminals were easily pardoned at this

---

[14] Psalm 83

time, providing they were willing to volunteer to serve as mercenaries in the war against England: their old ways lingered within them even in times of truce. They consistently fell back into their vicious life-styles. Aristocrats were set upon; desperate and deliberate pillagers were everywhere.

Visible fires were set just to burn the bodies that had been consumed by the Plague. The scent of burning flesh was nauseating, and remained as a memory in the nostrils of the survivors forever. There were particularly virulent outbreaks of this Pestilence in 1374, increasing the chaos and despair in the streets.

In the midst of this calamity, the townspeople were primed for revolution. They were enraged by the ever-increasing burden of taxes, both during the time of Charles V and after his death, under the direction of the greedy Regents. These Regents were each further competing with each other, seeking to gain their own fortunes off the backs of the people.

Paris itself, its population dwindling from the 300,000 at its peak time, was really a collaboration of three distinct cities: the commercial city on north side of the Seine, where many resided, was crowded and felt to be without air, as well as without water. The area around Notre Dame and the Palais de Justice was the second city of Paris: from here the administrative decisions were announced. All these difficulties occurred under the vigilant gaze of the professors and the clerics of the University of Paris, the third 'city' of Paris. For a considerable time they had been in competition for power with the authorities; they could always act with impunity as they could claim clerical exemption if charged with any infraction. The University of Paris, with its thirty-nine colleges, was The Authority on Theology (and by derivation on Church law) and Art. This position at the Centre of determining the 'Christian and Moral right' was jealously guarded, and enabled the professors to hold and expand their power, both ecclesiastical and practical. At first the University was complementary to the Church; later it took on greater strength and became the major challenge to the Church. The

University of Paris had power and stability, whereas the Great Schism (1378-1417) enfeebled the Church by the national political agendas that gave support to each of the Popes.

Two very important students at the University of Paris then completing law degrees in 1398, were Pierre Cauchon and Jean Gerson[15]. They were both outstanding scholars, and went on to study theology there after completing their law studies.

---

[15] became Chancellor of the University of Paris, later defended Christine de Pisan's position in respect of the *'Romance de la Rose'*

Chapter VIII

Charles VI and Isabeau de Bavière

-- from 1385 –

*'O God, the heathen are come into thine inheritance;
Thy holy temple have they defiled....'*[16]

Being the king, without the responsibility of administration, should have allowed Charles the luxury of developing, but in truth, it was only an opportunity for others to manipulate him.

It became evident that the young king would require a queen. He was, after all, in his seventeenth year.

It had been the wish of his father Charles V, that a match be found amongst the Germans, to bring about stability to France and to strengthen her position *vis à vis* the English. My husband Etiènne de Castel had been sent on a number of missions (much in advance) on behalf of Charles V, seeking a suitable spouse for the young king.

It was finally Philippe le Hardi, the Duc de Bourgogne who proposed her, Elizabeth of Bavaria. He had sampled her himself, instead of objectively having her virginity assessed. He had then negotiated with Duc Frederick of Bavaria, her uncle, and contrived that a meeting be arranged at Amiens

---

[16] Psalm 79

where she would be arriving on a pilgrimage. The Duc de Bourgogne had her portrait delivered for Charles to view. Philippe had determined that Elizabeth would be his perfect tool to manipulate the young king. As planned, Charles was immediately taken on seeing her likeness, and declared that if she was anywhere near as seductive as her portrait, that he would have her. Charles was impulsive.

On the 16th July 1385, she entered the hall at Amiens, followed by the Duchess of Bavaria (her aunt) and the Countess of Hainault who was charged with her instruction in court etiquette.

Elizabeth was very plain. She was small, with a pale face and a high forehead. She had dark eyes and a thick pug nose. Her hair was dark and plaited. She had a long torso and short legs. Her garments did not improve her lustreless image. Neither by her presence nor by her features, was she by any measure, attractive. She had a very large and sensual mouth, however, and Charles immediately began to imagine her kisses.

Elizabeth advanced to kneel in front of the King. He rushed to her, and took both her hands to assist her to rise. She lifted her face to him, and they looked deeply into each other's eyes. He was impatient with desire for her. He did not want to call her Elizabeth, the German form of the name; he chose the more intimate French equivalent for her: he decided then and there to call her Isabeau.

It did not matter to him that she was without dowry. It did not matter to him that her virginity had not been duly confirmed according to the royal rites. In fact, all he could think about was carrying her off to his bed, with kisses and embraces and generous caresses. He declared his most ardent love for her, despite her inability to understand a word he said. He could not wait; the engagement was announced. The marriage was set for the afternoon of next day at the cathedral at Amiens.

It must be mentioned, that a sign of danger had been noticed on the pathway that Charles took to meet the princess Elizabeth. It was Bureau de La Rivière[17] who saw it first. There lay the body of a dead crow, a very bad omen.

======================

The shortness of time was solely down to the impassioned impatience of the king. He could hardly wait the one day needed to decorate the chapel and prepare the wedding menu. Despite this short time allowed, the wedding was supposed to be a grand affair. The event should have been marked by extravagances that would reach the lowest peasant, and give joy to the entire country. However, very little of that occurred. The king did remember to provide a table for the local citizens to partake of the bounty so hastily assembled.

The ceremony took place at the cathedral of Amiens on Monday the 17th July 1385; the reception was held in the adjacent Bishop's palace. The attendance was more modest than would have been expected, including only the travelling entourage that had accompanied Isabeau from Bavaria, her parents and her uncle the Duc Frederick were present. Charles' uncle, the Duc de Bourgogne was there, as well as his brother Louis, and his court. Etienne de Castel and I were amongst the celebrants, as Etienne had been a key negotiator in finding the required match.

======================

The newlyweds spent the next three days together, surrendering to their passions, morning, noon, and night. They were interrupted only by meals and brief moments of rest. Their bodies were joined in the greatest of physical love, and their young hearts attempted to follow.

The young king was forever seeking to please his queen; he felt that the haste, which he had demanded for this wedding, made it necessary that he make it up to her, by plying her with gifts upon gifts.

---

[17] one of the courtège of assistants to the Duc de Bourgogne

After these three days, the Duc de Bourgogne interruped Charles' pleasures. The Flemish had attacked the Duke's lands; he portrayed this attack as an attack on France. Charles responded, by quickly going to the battle at Damme in Flanders. He arrived there on the 1st August, during the hottest period of the summer. He and the Duc de Bourgogne led the battle, wherein they were eventually successful despite the English support that the Flemish had gained.

Isabeau decided to leave virtually at the same time as her husband, after having visited the bishop of Amiens to convey her thanks that he had both performed the ceremony of marriage and offered a kind benediction. She asked for his prayers for the safe return of her husband, and also for her safe journey to the Château at Creil in Picardy, the first of her residences.

On the 25th September, Charles returned to Isabeau, at Creil, where they renewed their passions. The next day the young couple and the Duc de Bourgogne breakfasted together. The young king then departed with his uncle for Paris, whilst Isabeau went to the Château le Manoir de Beauté sur Marne at the edge of the forest at Vincennes, in the village of Nogent. Isabeau enjoyed the beauty and tranquillity of the place. She remained at Beauté and Charles returned to her on the 5th October, when he managed to stay for an entire fortnight, before departing for Champagne.

And so it continued: Charles was often absent. Isabeau remained most often in Paris, either at l'Hôtel St-Pôl or at Château Beauté sur Marne.

Isabeau learnt quickly to manoeuvre at court. In Charles' absence she found herself a variety of 'tutors' to teach her. She chose in particular Bois-Bourdon[18].

---

[18] member of the house of Bourgogne

BOOK III

The Court:

The words of an anonymous Onlooker

Chapter IX

Isabeau de Bavière and Bois-Bourdon
Louis, Duc de Touraine and
Valentina Visconti

-- from 1387 --

'The transgression of the wicked saith within my heart,
That there is no fear of God before his eyes.
For he flattereth himself in his own eyes,
Until his iniquity be found to be hateful.
The words of his mouth are iniquity and deceit:
He hath left off to be wise and to do good.
He deviseth mischief upon his bed;
He setteth himself in a way;
He abhorreth not evil...'[19]

Isabeau quickly realised that she had suddenly been planted in a prominent position in a dissolute, dangerous, and devious Court. It suited her spirit and captured her imagination, to learn the games of intrigue. She waited in excited anticipation as she began to plan her path to take advantage of these opportunities.

Among her entourage, she noticed one of the courtiers who

---
[19] Psalm 36

offered her homage. He was young and physically beautiful. He moved with strength and grace. He appeared to be a perfection in knighthood. Apart from that, he had power in his speech and clarity in his thought. He knew the answers to most of Isabeau's questions, even before she asked them.

She felt the excitement of seduction in his presence; lust blossomed within her. She neither could, nor wanted to, resist her attraction to him. His name was Bois-Bourdon.

Once, he came upon her in a corridor of the royal residence at Château Beauté sur Marne, near Paris. He boldly drew her aside and whispered to her: 'I love you, Isabeau. You are the most beautiful and powerful woman I know. You inspire me. You have held me under your spell since first I saw you. I must have you. Your frequently absent husband Charles is not worthy of your strength and your passion. You are ripe for the love I offer. Render your passion to me, and I shall be true to you alone.'

Isabeau was embarrassed that he had read her feelings; it made her feel vulnerable that he knew both her desire for him and her greed for power. She composed herself and answered him, concealing her blush: 'Friend, you are not capable of being true to anyone, but I am the same, so I cannot condemn you for the desire I share.'

Bois, at that instant impulsively drew her to him. They embraced and he quickly carried her to one of the many available bedchambers off this corridor. He undressed her deftly, and she responded to his experienced caresses. The diabolical pleasure of sin became the foundation of her conspiracy, a power which would reign from that moment onwards. The love-making served to cement some yet to be devised schemes.

'Madame,' said Bois, 'I want to advise you about the intrigues at court.' She answered flippantly, 'but you intrigue me also....what do you mean?'

'My dear Isabeau, you cannot reach your proper strength without understanding the conspirators who surround your husband, the King. By knowing who these conspirators are, and their weaknesses, as well as the weaknesses of the King, you will become the true power of France, and I alone can help you.'

Isabeau was aroused by the possibility of gaining control of the French court, and hence control of France. She felt that she was on the path of the unknown, but the path to power.

She responded to her new found lover and thought of how she would use him. 'I accept your proposal and assistance,' she answered, 'without the slightest hesitation,' pandering to his strength. 'I will involve myself and instigate disorder in the Court....' She looked at him with interest and intent, assessing the effect of her words on him. She added, 'I vow to use any manner or means to realise my ambitions....'

'The king is good, but very weak, and yet I am already able to control his weaknesses. I shall begin at once to implement our strategy.'

Bois watched her, he loved her. He was astonished and bewildered, all in the midst of lustful and unceasing lovemaking. He had become her instrument. He found himself, the seducer, being seduced. Clearly, he had met his match.

Isabeau went on: 'The Key to the Plan must be to eliminate the three Regents. But first we must gain the support of Louis, the King's brother.' Bois-Bourdon answered her in surprise: 'why must we involve him? You have me.' He realises that the Mistress had become the Master-Mind of the Plot to seize absolute power.

Isabeau continued: 'I do not mean to confuse you. It is true that Louis is young and filled with ardour and ambition, but most importantly he is filled with royal blood.'

Bois responded, 'You alarm me, Isabeau, I fear you. I loathe the idea of sharing you with anyone, even the King. I do not want a rival for your love and your passion. But I love you, so I accept whatever conditions you place on me. I shall be your eyes and ears, and your most loyal servant and strong supporter. Give me a sign of our pact, a ring perhaps... that I can carry near to my heart...'

Isabeau continued, 'No one could rival you, my Bois, but if I must, with cold reason, open my bed to other lords, and of course to the King, whom I control entirely, it will only increase my passion for you. I give you this ring, with my seal, that you shall wear on a chain around your neck.' Her boldness in giving him this secret token put her at risk, a danger which increased her physical excitement at this promise of unceasing sexual fulfilment and her future intercourse with power. 'Everyone in the court only thinks of taking money and indulging in pleasure. Surely, I as Queen, should not be deprived. Dear Friend, Dear Lover, Dear Servant of my body, I will always seek your advice. You are my kindred spirit. Kiss me, my Bois, on my lips and all over my body, again and again.'

Whenever Isabeau and Bois would come upon each other, in the court or in the corridors of Power, they were seen to exchange flirtatious, suggestive, lustful glances. The conspiracy between them began to organise itself into a political force without scruples.

================

Isabeau had thus begun to develop a strategy to become the strength behind the throne of France. In collusion with the Duc de Bourgogne, she managed to send Charles on a phantom campaign to Flanders. This was one of many expeditions that she organised to occupy him. She preferred to be left to rule the great household on her own. She sent him on expeditions of conquest and on various expeditions to support an end to the Schism of the Church. It was also her recommendation for him to keep the army well employed.

================

During Charles' absence, Isabeau organised an exquisite but intimate banquet and dance, to engage others as allies. Many of the most important courtiers and their ladies were invited;

she invited her brother-in-law, Louis duc de Touraine, to sit by her side as she presided over the gathering. She herself was richly dressed for this grand performance, and provocative as the powerful hostess. Louis was even more handsome than she had noticed before; he was tantalisingly seductive. He was normally confident with the ladies of the Court as he had already seduced many. Isabeau, his sister-in-law and queen, however, was another matter. Bois-Bourdon hungrily watched her every move from the other end of the table.

The dinner was beautifully served; the queen toasted her absent husband, and wished welcome to all. The trumpeter blew his note to announce that the dancing would commence. All eyes turned towards the queen who offered her hand to her brother-in-law. They rose and began the dance. The others followed.

The dance was slow and languid. Suddenly Isabeau appeared faint and flushed. She leant heavily towards Louis, and whispered. 'Dear Louis, I feel unwell. Take my arm and move me away from the crowd.' They withdrew to the veranda where darkness shrouded their intimate conversation.

'I thank you for rescuing me from that conniving group of parasites. I apologise for having put you through all this boring torture. I feel that we must outwit these people. They seek not to serve France but to pillage her.' Isabeau noticed the look of surprise on Louis' face. She continued, 'will you help to remove them and reconstruct the Court? They do us no good, and they serve only at the behest of the three Dukes, the uncles who have denied both Charles and you of your rightful inheritance.'

Louis answered, with astonishment in his voice, 'Isabeau, *ma Reine*, I had not known until this moment how perceptive you are. You are correct about the uncles; we must find a way for them to be relieved of their responsibilities.'

'It is agreed. But now dear Louis, you must know that your brother Charles, who is my kind and gracious husband, is weak. It is truly you, dear brother-in-law, who should occupy the throne of France.' Isabeau took hold of his hands and gazed deeply into his eyes. 'Now I also admit, freely to you. It is you I fancy; I have been in love with you since the day I first saw you. I can confess this only to you.

'It is lonely to be a queen, particularly in the light of your brother's delicate mind. I seek only your help and your love.' Isabeau drew Louis closer, and began to kiss him.

'Isabeau, dear Isabeau, this is more than I could have imagined. I desire you unreservedly. I give you my support to expose the regent uncles and strip them of their power. As for my brother the king, he can wear the crown for now, as long as you are here. You wield the strength.' He yielded to her, he kissed her passionately. She led him to the same bedchamber that she had shared with Bois-Bourdon. Bois followed them with his eyes, feeling pangs of jealousy about their destination, but balancing this jealousy with the knowledge that this union with Louis in the bedchamber was required to engage his energies in their conspiracy.

The next morning of this extraordinary alliance, Isabeau and Louis awakened early. Isabeau seemed to be a woman in love. She touched his cheek and said 'I have not dreamt your love. You are here beside me. '

'Of course I am; you now rule my heart. Now that I know that our interests are the same, we are permanently aligned.'

In truth, Isabeau was not in love with anyone: she was only in love with Power.

==========

Influenced by Isabeau and Louis, Charles VI convened a meeting in Rheims in 1388. In attendance were the Dukes of Berri, Bourgogne, and Anjou, as well as Charles' maternal uncle, Louis de Bourbon. Also present was the Cardinal de Laon and some of his associates. The cardinal rose and opened the meeting. 'I believe that we have an opportunity to profit from this occasion,' he said, 'to beg Charles who has now attained the age of twenty years, to rule over us on his own.'

This declaration was met with total enthusiasm by all apart from the regent uncles who departed rapidly in anger.

The day after his pronouncement, the cardinal was found dead, poisoned by an unknown hand.

Thus Charles VI inherited a country bankrupt of money, land, and national treasures.

He did come into his own, however, making many official changes at court, bringing back the advice of the Marmosets including the notable Bureau de la Rivière, seeking to rule according to the kind pattern of his father. From the previous Court, he retained his maternal uncle the Duc de Bourbon. He bestowed honour, power, and special privileges on his brother Louis, in appreciation of his support in ridding the court of the burden of the uncles. Bois-Bourdon remained at court, as did the Marquis Pierre de Craon, the best friend of Louis. Isabeau employed a great new staff to increase her own importance: servants were engaged to pamper her. Designers and dressmakers and jewellers were brought on board to commence the frantic activities to prepare for the moment of her coronation.

Isabeau maintained her affair with Louis. At about this time, when Charles was seeking to become more of a king, she needed to improve Louis' position, for her own purposes. She took him to her bedchamber, and after passionate love-making, she said, '*Cher Louis*, I have been thinking that you must now find a wife, to diffuse any notion of our deep relationship. I have given this predicament serious thought. I have come upon the ideal choice for you: Valentina Visconti. She is the daughter of Gian Galeazzo Visconti, Duke of Milan, and Isabelle de France, your aunt, thus a relation to both of us. I propose that you make your intentions known, and begin to court her.'

Louis pondered, and answered, 'I will have a cousin for my wife, my sister-in-law for my mistress, and our relationship can remain as vital as it is, yet unseen.'

Isabeau smiled, and said, 'I can continue to be a good and dutiful wife to your brother and as ardent with you as always.

My husband still adores me. The great tenderness he conferred upon me since we first met, has not dimmed. He loves me not only with his heart, but also with all the passion of his body. I am grateful for that. For if I have a child quickening within me, it could be his, but most probably will be yours. The son of a king, if he can father one, will not necessarily be king, but my son will, and my darling, he might be yours.'

Chapter X

Marriage of Louis, Duc de Touraine and Valentina Visconti

Coronation of Isabeau de Bavière

-- 1389 –

*'O come, let us sing unto the Lord:
Let us make a joyful noise to the rock of our salvation.
Let us come before his presence with thanksgiving,
And make a joyful noise unto him with psalms...'*[20]

Valentina was as fair and good, as Isabeau was dark and evil. She was thrilled at being courted by Louis. She succumbed to his charm and good looks, and was enchanted that he had chosen her. She was not aware of the conspiracy that she was entering. They were married by proxy in 1387, which allowed Valentina's large dowry to be assembled. This further gratified Louis.

With her came an escort of 1300 knights, looking after her on her journey over the Alps. Her trousseau was of indescribable beauty and luxury. One of her robes, for example, was dripping with thousands of pearls and diamonds.

---

[20] Psalm 95

She brought with her exquisite furnishings and fabrics, far surpassing any others in the realm. She was a cultured person, highly intelligent. She spoke fluent Latin, French and German, as well as her native Italian. Clearly, Queen Isabeau could not compete[21].

According to the plan agreed between Isabeau and her lover Louis, he married Valentina in person on the 17th August 1389. The wedding was discrete, as the following week would be the coronation of Queen Isabeau. The wedding paled in comparison.

The only opposition to this union was the extreme jealousy of the duc de Bourgogne. He felt his influence at Court and over Isabeau diminishing, which greatly angered him.

Despite Valentina's obvious personal advantages, Isabeau welcomed Valentina into the royal household, making sure that Charles noticed her also. Isabeau was well motivated in this regard; if she could compromise Charles with Valentina, her affair with Louis would be less noticeable. Valentina was drawn to Charles, feeling his need and his loneliness in his demeanour, despite his majestic bearing.

=========

The coronation of Queen Isabeau was a sumptuous celebration, held just about a week later, commencing on the 22nd August at midday, when she departed from the Abbey at St Denis to proceed through Paris. The cortège entered Paris at the porte St Denis, where the Queen was greeted by drapes of light blue silk, studded with stars. Here young children dressed as angels, sang hymns, a living tribute to their Queen. The air was fragrant with the heady scent of flowers, especially lilies and roses. The sun was hot and the sky was blue. All the fountains offered wine instead of water.

On the 23rd August she arrived, surrounded by her entourage

---

[21] Isabeau's linguistic skills were marginal; she never lost her heavy German accent in her French.

at La Sainte Chapel, where joyous crowds as well as Charles awaited her. The coronation was celebrated with great solemnity; the heavy bejewelled crown was placed on her head. She wore this crown only briefly, as it was replaced with a lighter one for the continuing festivities. She was carried back to the Palais du Louvre on a litter, covered with silks and bedecked with flowers. A banquet was hosted for about six hundred princes and prelates, nobles and their ladies, from near and far. Food was heavily laden on golden platters, served onto golden dishes, wine drunk from golden vessels. Minstrels played melodiously. The princesses, including Valentina, and the aristocratic ladies, including Christine de Pisan, surrounded her throughout the event. They were all richly attired with jewels and garlands. After the meal, Isabeau departed for l'Hôtel St-Pôl by uncovered litter, so that all could view her. She was exhausted by then, because of the August heat and ceremonial attire, but most of all because she was seven months pregnant. She retired rather than joining the dancing that evening; Charles was, however, in great vigour, happy to participate in these pleasures.

On the 24th August, Isabeau received a great many of the townsfolk who presented her with an inordinate number of finely crafted gifts. Again there was a ball planned for the evening, and again she declined due to her condition. The feasting continued for a further three days, with jousting, tournaments, dancing and banquets for all. Finally on the Saturday, the 28th, the nobles and their ladies departed, enriched with the many presents they had received. The multitude of townsfolk were inebriated as a result of these celebrations. In the end, they were, however, bewildered by the addition of taxes required to fund them.

This was a moment of great heat and great excitement, but with an undercurrent of great fear, belying the official joy.

======================

Isabeau travelled with Charles and Louis to Vincennes, and stayed there with her young daughter Jeanne[22] and with Valentina. Charles departed soon after with his brother and their uncle, the duc de Bourbon for Avignon, to lend his support to ending the Schism. Pope Clement VII received them with great pomp. The Pope feted them with great banquets and profane joys provided by the company of far from holy courtesans. Charles also went away with a plethora of Indulgences, but practical resolution to the problem of the Schism did not occur. Pope Clement had made Charles VI his ally by bawdy entertainment and absolution therefrom.

====================

Isabeau returned to the Louvre in October for her confinement. Her baby, Isabelle, was born on the 9th November. The message that a daughter had arrived, reached Charles at Avignon shortly thereafter. He was disappointed not to have fathered another son, and continued his travels instead of returning home. He went to Nîmes, Montpelier, Béziers, Narbonne, and Toulouse. He was well received throughout, but particularly in Montpelier, where naughty ladies were available. Like his brother, he was noted for his carnal appetites. He and Louis finally returned exhausted, to Isabeau and Valentina in Paris in early January 1390.

====================

From then on, according to Isabeau's plan, the royal relations resumed and continued, in the various royal residences, between the King and Valentina, and between Louis and Isabeau. Isabeau held the power of manipulation over all; she began to utilise a variety of drugs to control her husband, his swinging moods were in her hands.

She presided over this Court of lust, and used it with selfish

---

[22] Second child of Charles VI and Isabeau, born in 1388, died in January 1390, see Appendix.

purpose. Upon his return, she came to her husband's bedchamber and seduced him with the required flattery and tenderness. She spoke softly to him, saying, 'Charles, I have missed you, my darling. It is your love-making I require.'

He was delighted with this turn of events, and undressed himself and Isabeau quickly. He was thoroughly enraptured, responding to Isabeau without suspicion. Her face was like a masque; he could not see her thoughts. She continued to charm him sweetly, whilst calculating. They made love with considerable passion, an area in which she had become well skilled. As he was satisfied, she began her next campaign.

She said, 'Charles, my Charles, I have been thinking about your power over France... We are besieged on one side by the Armagnacs, and on the other by the Burgundians... I think that to guard our royal family, it might be a wise move for you to increase the stature of your brother, Louis, duc de Touraine, by ceding the lands of Orléans to him... and giving him the title, Duc d'Orléans.....'

She kept him calm; she convinced him to do as he was asked. It was already nearing the middle of 1392.

BOOK IV

Catharine's story:

Lives are joined

Chapter XI

Catharine and Marie La Lapine and Christine de Pisan

- from August 1389 -

*'It is a good thing to give thanks unto the Lord,
And to sing praises unto thy name, O most High:
To shew forth thy loving kindness in the morning,
and thy faithfulness every night.......
O Lord how great are thy works!
And thy thoughts are very deep.'*[23]

I, Catharine, was truly thriving in the serene atmosphere of Poissy. The ordered environment continued to make me feel secure. I even enjoyed looking after my playmates, who were all of very high birth or of royal lineage. From time to time, I had a few moments of loving education from my mother who wanted me to continue to develop my abilities and knowledge of herbal healing. I learnt how to unlock the powers of the different plants from the garden, using either the flowers, the stems, the leaves or the roots for very specific purposes. Some elements were cooked, others were ground by mortar and pestle, others were scraped or shaved. Some plants exuded extracts, looking almost like milk.

---
[23] Psalm 92

My mother was accepted in the convent, not as a nun, but as the keeper of the herb garden and the infirmary. I was allowed to stay with her at the beginning, and then was moved into the dormitory where the very young girls stayed. I really worked there, helping them get dressed, and teaching them some of the little songs I knew.

When they went to lessons, I was allowed to accompany them. I expected that learning would be much as it had been at Montpelier, where my classmates were the foundlings that had been left at the convent gate. Here, however, different comportment was required, in the company of the high born. My native enthusiasm was so great that I participated too vigorously communicating my thoughts, disrupting these young children, nearly taking over the class. Dame Marie summoned my mother and spoke seriously with her on the subject of me.

She said, 'your little Catharine is far too enthusiastic in her pursuit of the joys of life. I had feared this when first I met her, noticing her bounding gait and her bouncing golden curls. I was hopeful that her natural vivacity could have been calmed by the serenity of Poissy. I regret that our environment does not really suit her. As you know, you have already proven your worth to this convent. You are essential here.

'I propose that we find an alternative way for your Catharine to develop. I have given this possibility some thought, and will give you a letter to introduce her to Mme Christine (de Pisan) Castel. Her husband, Etienne de Castel of Picardy, is in the service of the King, my nephew. They will receive you.'

With this letter, we were despatched towards Paris. It was still summer, just after the middle of August, as I recall. The convent allowed us two mules and a guide to escort us in safety to Mme Christine's residence.

=====================

As it turned out, we entered Paris in the midst of the jubilation underway, celebrating the coronation of Queen Isabeau. There were horses and people and flowers and garlands everywhere. The heady fragrance of flowers, mingled with the sweating bodies of the populace, and the vapours from the free-flowing wine, nearly stopped my breathing. There were shouts of *'Noël, noël!'* which I did not understand. Our guide lifted me up, so that I could see better, but with wave upon wave of intoxicated people, I could not comprehend what was occurring. In the end, our guide enabled us to find our way through the festivities to the Castel residence; without him it would have been impossible even with the best directions. I felt calmed by him, fearless despite the total divergence from anything in my previous experience. It was quite disorienting for my mother, as she was unaccustomed to the excesses which were offered. Her Cathar ways kept her quiet and very sober throughout our progress.

Stepping over the dying flowers from the coronation, and the piles of debris that resulted from these celebrations, our guide finally brought us to the home of Christine de Pisan, which was not far from the Louvre. She lived in her city house at that moment[24]. She had just arrived home after the jubilations.

My mother presented the letter of introduction to the servant who opened the door, and we were admitted into Christine's study. It was a wondrous place, filled with huge volumes of books, bound in leather. I was truly impressed by the spirit of learning that I felt when entering. I touched her desk; I felt the wood of her chair, and felt wholly immersed in the sanctity of knowledge, without knowing what the knowledge might be.

Christine entered the room. She was simply attired, wearing a long blue dress of silk. The neck was low, fitted precisely over her breast. The dress was tapered at her waist. Her outer sleeves flowed, whilst her inner sleeves which were richly embroidered, were tight to her wrists. She wore a large gold

---

[24] Her father had been given this house by Charles V. Christine had inherited also another, called Orsonville, in the southeast of Paris.

brooch at the neckline of her dress. Her elegant white wimple framed her oval face, which appeared both wise and kind. I couldn't take my eyes off her. Her eyes met mine and she smiled at me; I was in awe. I gazed down at my simple homespun linen dress and apron, and wondered if I might ever achieve such understated elegance as that of Madame Christine.

My mother and I curtseyed deeply when we saw her. She read the letter from Dame Marie and looked up. She stared at me again; I felt certain that she saw some of herself in me. (I hoped so.) She ignored my mother for the moment, and spoke directly to me.

"Catharine, " she said, "how old are you?"

"I am nearly nine," I answered.

"And what do you enjoy, Catharine?"

"I love life, and I love my Mother. I love all God's seasons and all God's creatures. I love hearing the bells chime at the convent, so that I know what time it is, and what I must do. I love the gardens, the smell of flowers and herbs." As I could no longer contain myself, I burst out, "I think you are beautiful, Madame Christine. I want to learn from you." With that enthusiasm, I rushed to the books on her shelves, just to touch them. I nearly felt that knowledge would work its way through my fingers!

Just at that moment, another little girl, of approximately my age, appeared at the door of Madame Christine's library. It was Madame Christine's daughter. I was delighted at the prospect of being with her. I rushed to tell Madame Christine this thought.

Madame Christine, looked up, and called to her daughter. "Come in, come in... There is someone I want you to meet. Marie, this is Catharine."

Marie answered, "Catharine, I am pleased to meet you. I heard your voice chattering in the room, and was curious."

"Good day," I said, "I am so pleased to meet you. I hope we can be friends. I know lots of things about plants and flowers, and I'm sure that you know many things that I do not know."

Christine smiled, and turned to my mother. "Madame," she said, "I now understand the tone of the letter from Dame Marie. She has asked that I take your Catharine as my ward, and that you return to Poissy where you are needed. I see that your Catharine is gifted, enthusiastic, and adaptable. I welcome her to our household, and am pleased that she will truly be a suitable companion for my daughter, who is just a little bit younger."

My mother and I were invited to stay the night there together. I would be given a more permanent bed the next day, and my mother would return to Poissy.

But first we were bid to dine. Madame Christine's maid came to fetch us from the library. We entered the hall where a large trestle table was laid with a white cloth and on it were bowls filled with chicken broth, pasta and almonds. It smelled delicious, and I was really hungry by then. We said grace. The maid brought some warm fresh rolls; they were swollen and puffy: I always delighted in newly baked bread. Madame Christine and my mother drank wine, whilst Marie and I drank fresh milk. I was so grateful for this hearty meal, and felt truly replete. When the maid cleared our dishes, I got up and tried to help her, but was told to sit instead. Another maid followed her, and brought in the dessert, to which I was unaccustomed. We were given fried fig pastries which were flavoured with honey and spices. It was really good.

After the meal, Marie took me by the hand and showed me the house, which to my eyes, was very grand. As it was not yet dark, we also walked in the garden together. I was very excited to see so many plants growing there. I named them all, and she was very impressed. She had lived with them, but didn't know their names, or anything about their healing properties. But in the end, we were able to sing some songs together, before we went back inside.

At her invitation, my mother spoke to Christine about her interests. She explained about cures, using the plants and spices which grew wild in the countryside, as well as those in tended gardens. She convinced Christine that proper selection of herbs could be very healthy for one's body, in addition to their property to add taste to food.

Christine was sympathetic to the fact that my mother was a widow, having lost her husband in a most dreadful way. My mother explained, without mentioning Stephen, about our perilous journey, coming all the way from Carcassone, via Montpelier, to Poissy and now finally to Paris. She understood why my mother, with all her skills, had been so readily accepted by Dame Marie at Poissy.

At last my mother and I said 'Good night' both to our hostess and her daughter Marie, and to each other. I knew that this would be our last night together for a very, very long time. I hugged her tightly. I felt her body close to mine. I nuzzled against the nape of her neck, and breathed in her lavender scent. Although it was a warm night in August, I needed to be as close to her as I could ever be. 'I love you, *Maman*, you are not only beautiful, you are brave. *Tu es bonne... Bonne nuit, Maman.*'

My mother asked me to pray with her: '*Je vous salus, Marie, Mère de Dieu.*' She removed her rosary, the very one received from Dame Elizabeth, from her neck and placed it once again on mine. The carved rose felt cold against my skin.

Chapter XII

Catharine and Christine de Pisan

Death of Etiènne de Castel

-- 1389 - 1390 --

'Lord, who shall abide in thy tabernacle?
Who shall dwell in thy holy hill?
He that walketh uprightly,
And worketh righteousness,
And speaketh the truth in his heart...'[25]

My early days with Madame Christine were just as I had imagined and hoped. I sat with Marie every day and we did our lessons. Madame Christine taught me more about letters and spelling and sums. I was soon able to read enough that she allowed me to turn pages in her wonderful books. She taught me never to wet my fingers when I turned these precious pages, as the ink used was often poisonous.

Christine sought to increase our happiness by increasing our knowledge. I loved reading, not so much writing, but my little companion wrote beautifully. Our days were well ordered. We played enough, often in the garden; we prayed

---

[25] Psalm 15

enough. Madame Christine was not always serious. She smiled easily at our conversations, and laughed at our mischief. I think I loved her, nearly as much as my own mother. I was grateful for the wisdom of Dame Elizabeth for sending us to Poissy. From Poissy, the kind words of the royal princess Dame Marie had opened these doors for me, which would, eventually, give me access to the highest in the land. I remembered where I had come from: our tiny burnt shop in Carcassone was distant, but my early childhood roots would be forever there.

My experiences at Montpelier and at Poissy were of real value to me in this household. Although I was well treated by Madame Christine, I was given responsibility to look after her younger children. Her two little boys were delightful and very energetic, but not as interested in learning as Marie and I were, but then the eldest was only four. Learning about court comportment became very important, both for them and for me.

==============

Monsieur Etiènne de Castel was as handsome and elegant as Madame Christine had said. I found him truly engaging. We had the most wonderful evenings together, we girls singing and reciting for him after the evening repast, and after the little boys had been put to bed.

But what bothered me was his surname. I remembered a Guillaume de Castel from Carcassone. I had heard his name mentioned in hushed tones, by my parents. I was certain that he also believed as my family had, in faith. I had not heard this name since our departure from Carcassone.

One evening, Monsieur Etiènne was resting after a heavy day in the service of our King. I was alone in the room with him; my chores were done. I shared with him my memory of someone whose surname was the same as his. He was quite surprised. He asked how I knew him. I told him that Guillaume de Castel was a very important and wise person in our community in Carcassone. I lifted my Rosary (Rosaire), which had on it a Rose instead of a Cross, and showed it to him. "*Mon nom est Catharine...*" I said.

He looked at it, he acknowledged it, and remained silent. I put it back around my neck under my tunic, holding it close to my heart. The gold rose had suddenly gone cold, as I felt it next to my skin.

That moment never came again, but I knew from the look in his eyes, that his trust had been earned, and I knew that I could never disappoint him.

===============

Most afternoons we walked on the Quai des Celestins close to Rue St-Pôl near to where we were told that the royal family lived, in comfort and in beauty in contrast to the coldness and severity of the Louvre.

Madame Christine had just received an invitation to visit her friend Valentina Visconti who was also staying at l'Hôtel St-Pôl, which was just near our normal walk. We followed her that afternoon, and were allowed entrance at the main portal. The Queen's Lady in Waiting, who was called Catherine l'Almande, ushered us children into the gardens whilst Madame Christine went about her business. We were delighted by the sight and the perfume of the gardens of lilies and roses. We children were further astonished by the distant sound of roaring. I asked Catherine l'Almande about the sound, and she took us all to what she called the 'zoo' that was on the property. I had never seen anything like it. There were enormous cats that lived in large cages; they were the source of these sounds. They appeared ferocious, not like any cats I had ever known. They were called lions and had come from far away, given as gifts to the King from kingdoms in the Near East.

After a short while, we were called indoors, where Christine was seated with the Duchess Valentina in her bedroom. We bowed and curtseyed deeply as we entered. Just then, her Majesty, Queen Isabeau entered. Everyone rose and we all bowed and curtseyed even more deeply than before. Valentina offered the Queen her imposing chair; Christine whispered to me a word of caution, that I was now in the presence of her Majesty, the Queen of France. The atmosphere became quite formal. It was making me nervous. The Queen settled herself onto the ornate chair. Valentina and Christine seated themselves on the *tabourets*[26] on either side of her. She noticed us, even though we were quiet enough to avoid such recognition, and, she asked us to sing. We hardly understood what she said because she spoke in a strange and heavy manner. I was told afterwards that it was because she was from Bavaria.

Marie and I whispered to each other, deciding upon a song suitable for this occasion. We quickly agreed, and were pleased to sing together:

> '*Sur le pont d'Avignon*
> *Sur le pont d'Avignon*
> *L'on y danse* …. '

After our grand performance, we were quite overcome by the praises we received. Madame Christine decided that it was time to depart, after this, our first encounter with the two noblest ladies of our land.

We curtseyed again and were on our way.

I kept thinking about these ladies. Valentina was so beautiful. She was fair. Her blue eyes were soft and she appeared kind. She was graceful and soft-spoken. She was exactly as I had imagined a Queen should be.

In contrast the Queen, although I cannot fault her reception of us, was not elegant in appearance. She was everything that the Duchess Valentina was not.

My exuberant commentaries on our afternoon as we returned were curtailed by Madame Christine, who reprimanded me about my lack of caution. "No one outside our household must know where we have been, nor whom we

---

[26] Backless seat, stool

have visited today," she said. We walked carefully in the street, avoiding the open drains. We held our lavender sachets just under our noses, to avoid the stench of the streets.

At home Madame Christine welcomed my comments and observations. She reminded me of all that my mother had taught me. It was right for me to share these thoughts with her within the house, but I must remain silent outside.

===============

After I had been there for about a year, my thoughts turned to my mother, and I was sad in a way, that I had not missed her very much. I had been surrounded by the warm Italian atmosphere that was ever present in this home. There was no fear here; there was no intrigue. There was always confidence that there was love in this place.

===============

I felt some unease at one point; I don't really know when it started. I had inadvertently overheard a conversation between Madame Christine and Monsieur Etiènne one evening, after he had returned from his duties at the palace. He was saying that there was quite a lot of concern about the health of our King. His moods oscillated greatly, from one moment to another he changed from being totally rational to being quite mad, according to his servants. His moods were aggravated by drink, at these times he seemed possessed. He sometimes responded with joy to the Queen, yet at the next encounter, he hardly recognised her; from time to time he actively hated her. Christine corroborated: both Valentina and Queen Isabeau had mentioned these concerns to her.

===============

It was the 29th October in 1390, I shall always remember. Monsieur Etiènne was called upon to accompany our King to

Beauvais. I was sad that day, I felt a heaviness in my heart, although I could not know the source.

Christine was concerned, as she had just learnt that this area of Picardie was rampant with the Plague. She cautioned Etiènne, but he put it aside, as he was obliged to take the journey.

Just over a week later, one of Etiènne's servants arrived back from the expedition. It was his sad duty to tell Christine that Etiènne had died suddenly on the 7th November 1390. Christine's fears about the plague proved correct. Etienne's body was burnt where he died, his ashes co-mingled with other victims of the plague.

Laughter and joy disappeared from the home. Christine was beset with sorrow, and distressed by debts that had accumulated without her knowledge. Her life and our lives in consequence, appeared to be marching towards an abyss.

Chapter XIII

Catharine and Valentina Visconti

-- 1391 - 1394 --

> 'In thee O Lord, do I put my trust;
> Let me never be ashamed:
> Deliver me in thy righteousness...'[27]

Christine became very sad and lonely. She turned to her friend Valentina Visconti for moral support during the year that followed. I watched their closeness increase, although they seemed to be wary of the watchful and jealous eye of Isabeau de Bavière.

Christine was continually torn between choosing a contemplative life and an active one. But as a mother, withdrawal to the contemplative life of the convent could not be her option. She had to provide for her three children and her mother, and she had no resources, only the burden of the legacy of debt.

She was fortunate to have the support of Jean Gerson, a professor at the University of Paris. He began to encourage her to take up her pen and write down her very wise thoughts and observations. She left the running of her household to her mother; she withdrew to her study and began to write.

---

[27] Psalm 31

She was still consumed by her love for Etienne, so her first volume was one of love poems, dedicated to him. These poems were very much appreciated, even in those days, when women did not write. It was wonderful to see her succeed with something, in the face of her grief.

I was there with her, ever aware of her difficulties, seeking to help as much as I could, in her household. I was already in my eleventh year and quite capable.

One afternoon, when I returned home with Marie, after our play in the palace gardens, I overheard the voices of Christine and her Highness Valentina, in deep discussion. They heard us enter, and called us into the parlour where they sat. We both curtseyed deeply, and behaved respectfully. Christine's daughter, having made her appropriate pleasantries, departed; Madame Christine bade me stay.

"We have been discussing your future, dear Catharine, and we have come to some decisions, " Christine said. "Tomorrow you and I will leave for Poissy, to visit your mother. I must speak with her alone about our situation. You will spend just a few days with her, because you will then move to the household of the Duchess Valentina, and help her in various ways. I have told her about your special gifts, and I am certain that she will help you to develop them. I shall miss you very much, but as you know about my circumstances since Monsieur Etiènne's passing, I am unable to provide for you any longer. I will follow your progress even though you are not with me, and I will visit you at the royal residence from time to time."

I cannot say that I was entirely surprised by this turn of events. I felt happy that my future would be in the radiant presence of the one person, Valentina, that I really thought of as 'my Queen.' I understood my path, and I accepted it. I went to pack my few belongings, in preparation for my departure to Poissy.

====================

I was excited to take another journey, and was looking forward to seeing again the familiar, safe environment that I had left just over two years ago. But I was truly looking forward to the changes my new life would hold.

On our arrival at Poissy, we were received warmly by Dame Marie. Dame Marie was anxious for news about her nephews the young King Charles, and Louis, duc d'Orléans. She knew that she could count on Christine to give her the truth; the filtered information that she otherwise received was never precise, and filled with innuendo. She was concerned because she knew that Charles had inherited the mental weakness of the Bourbon family, and she was worried about his health. The rumours that reached her at Poissy did not comfort her.

As I silently stood there, in the midst of all of these questions, Dame Marie suddenly seemed to notice me. She directed me to seek out my mother in the garden.

Dame Marie spoke quietly to Christine, offering personal condolences for Etienne's sudden death, noting also that his vigilant presence at Court had served well both her brother-in-law Charles V and her nephew Charles VI. Then she spoke about the future. She entreated Christine to apply her talents to the task of honouring the memory of Charles le Sage, by writing his life story. Dame Marie, like Gerson, encouraged her to write more, both to give advice to women, and to share her poems. She said, "Your talent will support you; your fortunes will change."

"Now, Christine," she said, "we must discuss Catharine. I understand that you and Valentina have decided that she will move to l'Hôtel St-Pôl when she leaves here. I trust that you have apprised Valentina about her special gifts with plants and herbs and healing which she has inherited from her mother. I imagine that with some training, she could become very useful to the royal household, as her mother has become here."

====================

I found my mother at Poissy, much changed. She was not distant. I saw a new light in her eyes, the enlightenment of spirituality. She was content. I understood immediately that her way of life was becoming increasingly as that of a *Parfaite*. With outstretched arms she embraced me, pressing me close to her heart. The fragrance of lavender brought a flood of memories to my mind. She whispered, "my Catharine, our paths have now diverged. I am now protected from the ways of the world outside of this convent. I am at peace. But you, my beloved Catharine, I understand that you are moving to a royal household; I cannot help you there, but trust that the lessons you learnt as a child, will. I heard from Dame Marie about the death of Madame Christine's husband. I was worried at the time, but have prayed for a new solution for you. My prayers have been answered. I know from Dame Marie that the royal Duchess Valentina will need you. You will be her ray of sunshine. No matter where you are, you will always be in my prayers."

Now my mother tended her plants as she had tended me. Her garden was filled with the most exquisite poppies, in red, pink and white. She tended them with great care, as they were fragile. Where their petals had dropped, the soil was covered with a carpet of vibrant hue. She pierced a small hole with her knife into the fruit, enabling her to extract the milky substance, and allowing the seeds to be collected. She worked in her garden from morning until nightfall. When night came, she prepared her elixirs and ground seeds into powders with her mortar and pestle. She then stored them in perfect vessels, ready for final preparation as needs arose. She slept little, she prayed as she worked, she barely stopped to eat. The bells reminded her of the hours that passed, but did not govern her routine. Nature did that. She seemed closer to life as a *Parfaite* in the enclosure of the convent, where no one seemed to notice her true faith.

My mother had taken a vow of silence for most of her time, making only rare exceptions. Her retreat from the world was a retreat from me as well. She gave me her blessing, and sent me on my way, counselling me, 'Follow the path of your life. Give joy wherever that path takes you.'

Christine stayed on at Poissy for a few days. She remembered that my mother was also a widow in tragic circumstances, and felt that there was much they might share.

Servants arrived from the household of the Duchess Valentina to collect me. I left the gates of Poissy with a mixture of sadness, joy, and anticipation in my heart.

=================

It was already late autumn when I arrived back in Paris. I was taken directly to l'Hôtel St-Pôl where the Duchess Valentina was residing with the rest of the royal family. I did not know what to expect; but after my time with Madame Christine, I felt confident that I could adapt.

I was given some tasks to do, helping with some of the smaller children that were about. Then the Duchess Valentina had me brought to her bedchamber.

I remembered the enormous bed in the enormous room from my previous visit in the summer. Now a huge fire crackled. There was a pot hanging over the fire, and in that pot there were herbs which spread their perfume throughout the room. I could smell the scents of lavender and geranium. I felt enveloped in an atmosphere of sheer contentment. Valentina was propped up on cushions of embroidered satin. Her little dog was at her feet on the bed. Her new baby was in her arms.

Valentina beckoned me to come near. She indicated a little stool near her bed for me to sit on. She told me that Madame Christine had mentioned to her that I was very good with small children, and that I knew my letters and many songs. She allowed me to hold her new baby Charles, her first son and heir. I looked upon his sleeping face and began to sing one of my songs, which soothed him. It was at that moment, when I held him, and looked up to see the eyes of Valentina caressing my face, that I knew that my life's work would involve the care of children. Christine had opened my mind to the power of poetry; Valentina had opened my heart to care for children.

I discovered in a very short while, that I was to be her constant little companion. At the grown-up age of eleven, I felt like a little sister to her. Of course, I responded immediately to her every need.

As before, in Madame Christine's household, I found my way to the herb garden, and assisted in tending the plants there. But my path was changing; I was not to be responsible for cultivation.

It was not long after my arrival at l'Hôtel St-Pôl that Valentina made a decision about my education and my future. My love for children, was now a driving force. Valentina introduced me to Jeanne La Goutière, the chief royal midwife, and I began my training with her.

Jeanne La Goutière was a practical woman, large and matronly in appearance, a bit loud and rather coarse, but very, very efficient. She always wore a large white apron and a white head-dress. Her skirt was usually tucked into her belt. I watched her every move, but that did not perturb her. She was accustomed to having helpers around her; I was just an available pair of hands to assist her. I seemed to be naturally gifted in this area; I was always ready, offering exactly what was needed when it was needed. I boiled the water and presented the towels, which I saturated with the various healing herbs. It was as if I was attached to her in a way, helping with the births. I did not like her, but I did respect her and was grateful for the learning that she imparted.

During my first few months with Valentina, I assisted her with her baby. Then I would run rapidly through the palace to find Jeanne La Goutière and follow her round to deliver the infants of many within the royal household.

There was always a great deal of traffic in the corridors of power. I didn't really know how babies were conceived; I just knew about their arrival. I soon understood that these corridors were really just like rabbit warrens, and those I had observed first hand in Montpelier and in Poissy.

My days in my new environment were unceasingly active. They were filled with charm and intrigue, happiness and hell. I discovered that every corridor of the Court was filled with whispers, threats, and criminal intent. The only innocence was in the eyes of the children, which confirmed my desire to dedicate myself to their care.

I overheard various conversations as I passed through these hallways. I saw the large shadow of pregnant Queen Isabeau entering one of the bedchambers as I scurried after Jeanne La Goutière. The Queen was followed by a courtier called Bois-Bourdon, I learnt afterwards. I heard their voices, softly speaking to one another, and then her screaming in passion. I mentioned this to Valentina, and she cautioned me never to divulge any of my observations to anyone but her. She told me only, that there were many scandals surrounding the Queen and the Court.

It was soon after the beginning of the new year, 1392, that I was summoned to accompany Jeanne La Goutière at the birth of a new baby. We entered Queen Isabeau's bedchamber, and set about to the task at hand. We delivered her child, who was named Charles, on the 6th February, 1392. He was the long awaited Dauphin; I was really impressed to have been present at this royal birth.

Joy permeated the palace with this miraculous arrival. All Paris celebrated. It appeared that the Queen's power had been enhanced. The King was officially relieved to have an heir.

My life continued in this way, an invisible presence in the palace.

===================

After the intimate encounter of birthing her baby, I was relegated to again observing Queen Isabeau from a distance. I was frightened of her, as she berated everyone around her, even whilst she was giving birth. She did not appear to me, to have any Spirit of Goodness within her. I told Valentina that I had seen her husband, Louis, duc d'Orléans, in earnest conversation with the Queen, but Valentina was not surprised.

From time to time, Valentina was summoned to our King. She always took with her certain herbal preparations, which he needed. I saw what she took: the infusions she carried were known to me. I knew that their purpose was to calm his tormented head, but I did not know why he suffered.

====================

I was always busy, births were frequent and I learnt quickly, occasionally delivering some babies on my own by the end of 1392, but never the babies of the most royal women at the palace. I often looked after the babies after they were born, and came later to see how they were getting on. I seemed to be gifted with a special touch; all of the infants I caressed, thrived.

When I was not attending the newly born, I was looking after other children. When I was not occupied with children, I was with Valentina. As she got to know me and trust me, Valentina shared many of her innermost thoughts with me. I remember her looking very alone and sorrowful one day, when she took me into her confidence. She expressed concern that her husband Louis was constantly unfaithful. She felt that the purpose of her marriage to him was more to do with the wealth of her family and the dowry her father had provided, than to do with the undying love he had declared.

My suspicions about Queen Isabeau were also confirmed by Valentina. The Queen demanded that Valentina be available to spend time with the King; probably this gave the Queen the access to Louis that she desired. I avoided the Queen as much as I could, as I could not risk her wrath.

But it was not too long before another of her babies arrived. I again assisted Jeanne La Goutière in delivering Isabeau's daughter Princess Marie, on the 22nd August 1393. It was a very hot and humid day, I recall; my principal duty on that day was to bring flannels soaked with cold water to cool the Queen's brow; then I had to run back again with boiling water to sterilise the utensils. This was a difficult birth, for a very difficult Queen.

I did not know why at the time, but this Princess Marie was offered to the Church at her birth. Her destiny would be at Poissy.

BOOK V

Charles VI:

Onset of the madness:

Notes from an Anonymous Chronicler

Chapter XIV

Charles VI – The Madness

-- 1392 - 1394 --

'Give not thy strength unto women, nor thy ways to that which destroyeth kings.'[28]

In the spring of 1392, Charles was stricken with a serious attack of convulsions and fever. The doctors thought that he was suffering from an acute attack of typhoid. As soon as the fever abated, he lost nearly all his hair. His nails fell off. It was horrific. Despite these after effects, he took himself off on a hunt, in pursuit of one of his many avocations. As he was dismissive of his own illness, so were all those around him, including his doctors.

It was in the heat of the summer of 1392 that Charles' Constable, Olivier de Clisson, was attacked by numerous men, led by Pierre de Craon[29]. De Craon escaped to the safety of the Duc de Bretagne, an ally of Richard II of England. Charles was furious; in his mind, this was nearly an attack on his own person. The conflict between de Clisson and de Craon only increased: the crescendo occurred in a hand to hand battle in the streets of Paris, where de Clisson could have been mortally

---

[28] Proverbs, 31: 3
[29] landed, wealthy, devious, vengeful supporter of Charles' uncles, against the Marmosets; related to the Duchess de Bourgogne and the Duc de Bretagne.

wounded, but was saved inadvertently by falling into the doorway of a bakery, where the baker was attending to his tasks in the very early hours of the morning. Charles received the message of this event. In his night-shirt, he mounted his horse and galloped to the bakery, to hear in person the words of his constable. Charles wept at the sight of his injured supporter, mixing his tears with the blood of de Clisson. His ire increased; he declared that the Duc de Bretagne was his enemy. He ordered all of Craon's possessions to be confiscated; he ordered all of his residences to be razed to the ground; he ordered that his wife and his daughter should be imprisoned. These women were cruelly chased naked from their home and raped.

======================

Charles left for Palais St Germaine-en-Laye with his brother Louis. Charles was very happy spending midsummer there. Isabeau was distressed that Charles and Louis were enjoying their time together, without her. She was bent on disrupting this bit of sanity.

She sent a letter to Louis, containing a small sachet of yewberries. She instructed Louis precisely, mentioning the exact dosage to be administered to Charles, under the guise of protecting him from further attacks of madness. The contrary was intended; the contrary was the result. Isabeau also demanded that they leave their sanctuary and proceed to le Mans where his men of arms were gathering.

Louis, keen to comply with his Queen's wishes, yet concerned for his brother, gave Charles the drug, but in reduced dosages. Nevertheless, Charles' behaviour changed dramatically. He was dominated by irrational thoughts and random movements, visible to all. He suffered greatly, and Louis continued to administer the yewberries, carefully rationing the supply that Isabeau had given. As the supply diminished, the dosage was decreased and the King's health began to return. He was nearly normal by August.

A doctor had been engaged during his illness; the doctor declared to his carers that the King had been poisoned. This declaration fell on deaf ears.

Charles was again aroused to his demons on the 5th August as he returned from le Mans. He was on horseback in the forest when a tall, barefooted, bareheaded man in bleached, tattered clothing approached him directly, forcefully taking hold of the bridle of the King's horse.

'Proceed no further, my Noble Sire, ' he shouted, ' you are being betrayed.'

The King tried to continue his journey unaffected by these words, but could not. The party continued through the forest, suffering from the heat of the day. Charles felt this acutely: he was suffering from his indulgences of food and drink taken during the preceding days; he also wore a black velour cape, with a heavy scarlet hood that concentrated the suns rays into dizzy hallucinations.

Suddenly one of his soldiers dropped his sword, causing a very loud clatter in the otherwise quiet glen. The sound triggered fear in the King's heart. He started ranting and raving, 'I am being led to my enemies!' he screamed. He brandished his sword, attacking all those around him. Those who could flee, fled. His brother tried unsuccessfully to disarm him, and was injured in this attempt. His fury continued unabated until he had killed four of his own men, including a famous knight called Polignac de Gasgonne. At last his sword broke, giving opportunity to those around him to take over. He was bound up, and driven away exhausted, in a chariot.

The entourage finally arrived at Court in Paris at the Palais St-Pôl. Charles was carried in to Isabeau on a stretcher, accompanied by Louis. He spoke to her, 'My dear Queen Isabeau, I bring you your husband. Sadly he is totally unconscious and paralysed, as a result of the journey we first attempted earlier.'

'I thank you, Louis for bringing our dear King back to me. I have worried for his safety and for yours. I have anguished over his absence, particularly now as I know that I await the birth of yet another royal child. We must take all stress and worries from our Charles, allowing him to experience only joy. He will be surrounded by pleasures and happiness.'

The uncles viewed the incapacity of the King as their new opportunity. They again sought to become Regents: Isabeau would not have them in such an official capacity, but they did manage to replenish their personal coffers. It was of supreme importance to her that Charles should remain the peoples' *'Bien Aimé'*.

==================

As a part of organising pleasures for the King, Isabeau hosted a special ball at l'Hôtel St-Pôl for one of her favourite ladies in waiting, on the occasion of her third marriage, which in those days, would typically provoke ridicule rather than celebration. At the height of these festivities, wherein all parties were masked, a troupe of five men, all courtiers, disguised as hairy savages, made their dramatic entrance into the hall. Charles who was both drugged and drunken, insisted that he also participate in this charade and was attired accordingly. Their costumes were made from linen soaked in pitch. The men held hands and danced wildly, gesticulating obscenely. This was the famous Bal des Ardents. It was the 28th January 1393.

Louis passed by the savages much too closely, holding the flaming torch of one of his own courtiers. A spark from his torch ignited the highly combustible costumes, one after the other, until all the performers fell away. Two died on the spot; two others were carried off, to die later in agony. By a near miracle, the King survived. It was the young duchess of Berry, aged only 14, who noticed that it was her sovereign and threw herself onto Charles. Her voluminous skirts smothered the flames that attacked him. When the flames were extinguished, the King emerged, totally naked from under her garment, a glazed and bewildered expression on his face.

He seemed not to react to these events; he did not even

inquire about the fate of his fellow savages. From this time forward he lost memory of all basic things: he forgot to bathe and to attend to his bodily functions. He forgot his family; he was irritated by the sight of Isabeau. The only one who could approach him and calm him was Valentina. She attended him, mothered him as if he were an infant, and progressed him to the level of basic survival. She fostered his love, and remained his lover.

BOOK VI

Catharine's tale

Chapter XV

Catharine and Margaret

-- 1395 – 1397 --

The song of songs, which is Solomon's:
Let him kiss me with the kisses of his mouth; for thy love is better than wine.
Because of the savour of thy good ointment thy name is as ointment poured forth, therefore do the virgins love thee.
Draw me, as we will run after thee: the king hath brought me into his chambers:
we will be glad and rejoice in thee, we will remember thy love more than wine;
the upright love thee.

My life at the Palace continued with the birth of and care for babies, and also from time to time, of their loss. I was constantly on call to support the mothers and look after their little ones. All their needs were abundant. The secrets of these mothers were imparted to me, often under the stress of delivery, but also under the rituals of daily life. The network of sexual activity around the Palace was my normal knowledge. I ran through the corridors, from room to room, always attending someone. I was interested in all these people; they gave me a glimpse into another life, that I could only experience vicariously, not one that I could ever share.

I was again called upon to assist Jeanne La Goutière in late 1394. Queen Isabeau began her confinement well in advance of her next delivery, which was to be in the January. We scurried to and fro to support the Queen many days before, checking that she was in good health and prepared for this event. It was during these many demanding visits that I became well acquainted with Margaret.

Margaret looked familiar to me. She was a tall, fresh-faced wholesome countrywoman, very modest in her demeanour. I was taken aback when I entered the room and she greeted me with a smile: 'Hello, dear Catharine,' she said.

I might not have remembered her if I had seen her in the street, but her memory of me was quite astounding. She recognised me from the convent at Montpelier where she had last seen me. She had left the Hospice there shortly after my mother and I arrived. She had then joined a team of travelling midwives, always carrying with her a letter of her qualifications from Dame Elizabeth, referring her also to Poissy. She was ten years older than I, but our paths had followed much the same course. I remembered her now, she had regarded me kindly when I tried to fit in with the other children at Montpelier in 1385.

Margaret had been referred onwards from Poissy to the Royal Palace, because both Isabeau and Valentina, and indeed their entourage as well, were frequently with child. Dame Marie had mentioned me to Margaret and had asked her to look for me.

================

One afternoon we were hurriedly summoned to attend Queen Isabeau. We entered her bedchamber where she lay writhing against the satin sheets that had been brought to her from Venice. The room was dark, the heavy curtains drawn to keep out the cold. A fire crackled in her chamber.

She was naked and feverish, and suffering greatly. She

pulled me to her and demanded that I cool her brow. I ran for cold water and a flannel to place on her face.

Then Margaret told me to get the hot water. There was a cauldron boiling on the fire, so I ran to get it. When I got back, Margaret was coaxing the Queen's new baby from her body. There was not time enough for Jeanne La Goutière to arrive and supervise this delivery. There was a moment of trauma as the baby emerged. Margaret saw the problem right away: the umbilical cord was wrapped around its tiny neck. Margaret dextrously loosened the cord and delivered the baby girl. Isabeau heaved a sigh of relief that her prolonged suffering had ended. She declared that the delivery had been the gift of St Michael, in memory of the pilgrimage that she and Charles had made the year before, and declared the baby would be called Michelle. Before we took her away to care for her, she said to her baby, 'Michelle, you will marry and create an alliance for France.' Margaret took the new-born from Isabeau's hands, in readiness to take the child into another room to wash her and wrap her in swaddling clothes. As Isabeau was speaking, Margaret deftly handed me a basin, and told me to gather up in it, the afterbirth and the umbilical cord. I did as I was told, and I followed her.

Isabeau collapsed against the pillows, and her attendants took over.

===================

Margaret told me to place the contents of the basin into a small clean pot which was then set on the smouldering embers in the fireplace. All of the moisture evaporated from the pot. When it cooled, Margaret had me grind it into a powder. She wrapped the powder in vellum and placed it in a small leather pouch. There was a little powder left on her fingers; she touched them to the child's lips.

She baptised her, and then fell to her knees whilst I held the baby, and said the 'Our Father' nine times.

'But Margaret,' I said, 'this baby is healthy, not about to

die. Why have you baptised her now? And what is it that we have done with the afterbirth?'

Margaret raised her fingers to her lips and whispered, 'the Church would accuse me of sorcery if they knew of my actions. But the Holy Spirit guides me. I must protect each child that enters the world by my hands in the only way I understand. The powder from the afterbirth immunises; the baptism assures this baby of a place in Heaven; the 'Our Father' is the only prayer we really need.' Then, from under her garment she pulled out her rosary, where a rose was in the position where a cross could have been. The rosary was familiar to me, as it was much the same as the one that I had, that was given to my mother by Dame Elizabeth. Our Cathar faith united us more deeply than I had expected.

'Did you also perform this ritual when the Duchess Valentina brought her son into this world?' I asked.

'No, Catharine, I was not alone in the delivery room then. Jeanne La Goutière was present and in full charge. She took the baby away. I did quietly baptise this baby Charles on one of my visits to his cradle. Sadly I was unable to make use of the afterbirth on that occasion.'

==================

I had not thought about it whilst I scurried joyously round the Palace, but Margaret took it upon herself to point out to me her observations. 'Catharine, do you know that you cause a stir amongst some of the courtiers as you run from place to place, singing your little songs? I know that you are innocent, but your innocence brings a response from these men who watch you, increasingly with desire. Perhaps you should begin to think about your future possibilities, perhaps as a wife to one of the gentlemen attached to this Palace.'

'Margaret, dear Margaret, I had not thought about these things at all. I am at heart a joyous creature; I had my years of sadness and fear after I lost my father, but now I know that the worst situation of my life must be behind me. I greet each day with anticipation, happy to care for the little children and to visit the gardens. I really love my life. Marriage? I don't know, I feel some stirrings when the handsome knights gaze upon me. I know that normally I carefully retreat, not wishing to evoke any response.'

===================

By the time summer had come, I had become somewhat bolder. I actually spoke to several of the courtiers as they approached me, always with deference and politeness, of course. I began to think of Margaret's words, that marriage might be a real possibility for me. The following year I formed an attachment to one young courtier in particular, Robert d'Amiens. He was a squire to a knight in the service of Jean de Nevers, the eldest son of Philippe le Hardi, the Duc de Bourgogne.

Robert was tall and long-limbed. He was fair, with sparkling blue eyes. He came from the North, perhaps from Picardy. His aristocratic *Langue d'Aïl* accent charmed me, his expressions were so different and fascinating. I remember the first time he spoke to me: '*Où vas tu, ma Belle?? Et pourquoi si vite??....* where are you going, my Beauty, and why do you go so quickly? Wait a moment, and speak to me... please.... I want some moments of your time before I leave for the Campaign of Nicopolis against the Turcs.'

I couldn't catch my breath to run away. I felt compelled to respond to his words and his presence. I felt that he was the most handsome man I had ever seen. No high-born gentleman had ever spoken to me except to ask me to do a task... Robert asked nothing, just to speak with him.

All my normal chatter disappeared; I could not even think clear thoughts. I was under his spell. I just smiled, as words would not come. I felt my spirit connect with his; is this love, I asked myself? But I had no experience, and could not answer. I was grateful that he took over the conversation.

He told me his story in a way that made me feel close to him. He related his history, his family background, his courageous soldiering, his likes and dislikes, to me. I thought him perfect. I wondered why he had taken such an interest in me, generously sharing his soul. Could it be love?

I saw him every day for a whole month, yet managed to continue to fulfil all my duties. I told Margaret everything. She encouraged me; she found him to be an honourable person. I had no dowry, but Robert wanted me anyway. Robert said that the King had not required a dowry when he married Queen Isabeau, so why should he be any more demanding than his Majesty! Margaret found a priest to secretly marry us in early August. I informed Valentina and she advised me to ask Christine to stand in for my mother at the ceremony. Against her personal reservations regarding unions between members of different classes, Christine gave me her generous support, despite the strains in her own life. Valentina gave me the unexpected gift of a dowry.

We had several glorious weeks together, loving, kissing, being one. My body was his, my heart was his; his body was mine, his heart was mine. We were truly one; it was beyond anything that I had ever imagined. I had been an innocent child; now I was a woman aglow, loving every shared moment. Robert left at the end of the month.

I felt empty in his absence but still surrounded by his love. Margaret kept me occupied, filling my days with the familiar.

==================

'Until death do us part…'

On the 24th December 1396, during the Christmas festivities, disastrous news arrived at l'Hôtel St-Pôl. The Campaign had gone badly wrong in Nicopolis, and all had been lost. Jean sans Peur, as he was now called, with twenty-four Companions at Arms, was returning, after a large ransom had been paid. Only those few important persons were included in the group that had been spared. Ninety thousand of our Christians had been killed. The Parisians were devastated, knowing that their beloved King was in deep despair. So profound was his sorrow that he retreated into his madness; he remained ill until mid July of 1397.

I wept for Robert. Margaret comforted me. I wept some more. I was unprepared for this grief, a sorrow of such magnitude that it echoed the grief I had felt for my father and for Stephen. I had heard the attack on my father; I had witnessed the illness that took Stephen; I had not heard anything when Robert died. It grieved me that he was so far away when he lost his life.

I had been awaiting Robert's return with great anticipation, as it was now plain that I was carrying his child.

====================

It was quite an eventful time for Margaret and me at l'Hôtel St-Pôl. Queen Isabeau was again pregnant; and now I was also with child. I was grateful that we had previously taken Valentina into our confidence about my situation. I could have otherwise been dismissed in disgrace.

====================

It was January 1397 when we were again called to Isabeau's bedchamber for yet another winter delivery. The fire crackled; I lay lavender on it. The air was flooded with incense. Because it was winter, the temperature in the room was uneven, although we tried to keep the Queen comfortable. It was so difficult to satisfy Isabeau's many demands.

I was physically tired because of the child I was carrying, so Margaret took all of the difficult duties and allowed me the lesser tasks.

The baby arrived quickly and easily. Margaret took the child, handed him to me to cleanse him and dress him. Margaret tended the Queen, bathing her and dressing her in a silk night tunic, draping a shawl of gossamer wool over her shoulders. Margaret bathed her face in rose water and combed her hair. Isabeau then asked Margaret to assess her: 'How do I look, Margaret? Am I as beautiful as Valentina?' Margaret answered her carefully: 'My Queen you are beautiful. Your raven locks frame your face and you are radiant now, just after your child has been born. You astound and attract all those around you. You and Valentina are the most beautiful women in this Court.'

Isabeau was satisfied with Margaret's response, but seemed to anticipate something. It was clear that Isabeau was increasingly jealous of her cousin and sister-in-law Valentina. She had the attention of Louis her husband, but could not think beyond her own disadvantaged Bavarian background and was always competing, not only for attention as a woman, but also to gain power at every turn.

I was tending the young prince when Louis, duc d'Orléans, entered. It surprised me to see him there. But the child resembled him, I thought, rather than the king. I proceeded to bathe the baby and wrap him in the softest of cloths.

Margaret came to me and I handed the baby to her, so that she could show him. The Queen raised her eyes to meet Louis', and murmured: 'you, dear Louis, must be his Godfather, I will call him after you. He will be Louis, duc de Guyenne.'

I wondered how this beautiful baby had survived within the body of the Queen, with all her rumoured sexual antics.

We carried young Louis to the wet nurse, who was in the room adjacent. On our way, Margaret and I performed a secret baptism for the child.

Margaret suddenly turned toward me, and said, 'Perhaps Catharine, on the next occasion of a royal birth, you will not only assist as midwife, but also take the role of wet nurse. You are healthy and strong, and I am certain that you will produce abundant milk, not only for your child but enough to satisfy another as well.'

I was indeed grateful for the guidance and support I had received from Margaret, from Valentina, and from Christine. I thought of my mother, and would have liked to share some moments with her now, but knew that her life choice had made that impossible.

Chapter XVI

Catharine and Margaret

-- 1397 - 1398 --

Praise the Father, earth and heaven,
Praise the Son, the Spirit praise;
As it was, and is, be given
Glory through eternal days.

Valentina had been sent first to Asnières-sur-Oise, and then to Châteauneuf-sur-Loire in November 1396 by her husband. He was protecting her by keeping her out of Queen Isabeau's path. She had been falsely accused of sorcery because she had successfully calmed the King during his bouts of madness. Isabeau never succeeded in calming him, but then it is more likely that her use of various preparations would bring on his madness, not help him at all.

The news of these accusations reached the ears of the Duke of Milan, Galeas Visconti, Valentina's father. He was incensed when he heard it; he knew these accusations were false. He sent ambassadors to carry the message that he would wage war against France to protect his daughter's name. Valentina, sent her messages to her father, and calmed him, turning him from his harsh response, for the sake of the love she felt for her deviant husband.

By removing Valentina from the scene, Louis was also giving himself the freedom to remain Isabeau's lover. Valentina accepted the safety of this decision, in particular as she had her new baby Marie to look after.

It was early in the Spring of 1397 when Margaret and I were invited to join her there. Knowing that my baby would soon arrive, Valentina had made up some concerns about her baby that were plausible enough to warrant our attention and help. We were escorted by guards from the Orléans family. There were also some servants delivering supplies on this smallish expedition.

The weather was pleasant and our journey was uneventful. We arrived safely a few days after we left l'Hôtel St-Pôl, and were received in the customary way for persons of Valentina's household. We were shown to our quarters and refreshed ourselves. Then we joined our beautiful Valentina in her gardens. She was sitting there, surrounded by several of her ladies. It was peaceful.

Perhaps Valentina was feeling neglected in her exile, although we all knew that she was really much better off. The gardens were beautiful, and both she and her baby were thriving. I felt safe after having travelled through impoverished hamlets on our way. Need was abundant in the countryside; I was pleased to be an ordinary woman, not a royal personage.

I was very tired after this journey. Margaret recognised my symptoms. I was beginning some early labour pains, although I did not think of this: I thought I was just suffering from the jostling of the carriage. Margaret took charge; she got me a chamber with a large bed and clean sheets. Margaret gave me confidence and my labour was expedited. I responded to Margaret's commands, and watched myself respond to these commands as I had given them to many others before. Margaret deftly delivered my baby, whilst soothing my brow with a flannel scented with geraniums. 'You have a baby girl,' she said, placing my new daughter between my breasts. We thus allowed her to hear the beat of my heart from without, as she had previously heard it from within. Margaret cut the umbilical cord, and the baby began to suck. She had arrived beautifully and cleanly into the world. I saw Robert in her face and felt my heart tugged in sorrow, although I felt also his closeness at that moment. Hot tears of joy rolled down my cheeks, whilst Margaret bathed me. I asked Margaret to baptise my child directly in the Cathar way. Later I would have an 'official' baptism, and I would ask Valentina to be Godmother.

We said the 'Our Father' nine times, alternating phrase by phrase, our voices mingled.

Margaret said, 'Our Father '......I answered 'who art in Heaven'.... She said 'Hallowed be thy Name'..... I answered 'Thy Kingdom Come'......

I chose to name my lovely fair-haired daughter 'Christine Valentine' after the two women who I loved so very dearly, and who were so very important in my life.

Valentina came to see me after Margaret advised her that my baby had come into this world. Her kind warm presence filled the room. She turned gently to view my daughter, and smiled at me. 'You wanted to see me, Catharine?'

'Yes, my Duchess Valentina. I want to ask a great favour of you. I wonder if you would consider to be Godmother to *ma petite fille*.... I wish to call her Christine Valentine, after the two most important women who have helped me in my life....would that be possible for you? I would deem it such an honour ...'

'Yes, Catharine, I will take this honour that you offer... and I will advise you further. I will organise a baptism for your child here, and will place your Christine Valentine into the protection of the Orléans family. She will grow up with my daughter and with other children I may bear in future, much as you did in Christine de Pisan's household. We will see her disposition in time: if it suits her we may wish to place her in the care of the convent at Poissy...'

'Dear Duchess Valentina, I am forever in your debt. Your kindness and protection are unparalleled in this Kingdom.'

'You, Catharine, will have a further responsibility in my household. You will be wet-nurse for all of my future babies.'

====================

We stayed at Châteauneuf-sur-Loire for just over a year more. The little girls were very healthy and happy.

Margaret and I were recalled to Paris, in the summer of 1398, as Queen Isabeau was again beginning a confinement. Her son, Jean, was born in August 1398.

Chapter XVIII

Catharine and Bois-Bourdon

- 1399 – 1400 -

'...And lead us not into temptation...'

I settled back into life at the Royal Palace, but made frequent journeys to Châteauneuf-sur-Loire to see both Valentina and my little Christine Valentine. My little girl was well looked after and Valentina was the most kind protectress. She was always anxious for news of her husband, but knew better than to ask. His immoral behaviour and his use of her fortune, were two realities better left untold.

I curtseyed deeply to Philippe le Hardi, Duc de Bourgogne, on one occasion at l'Hôtel St-Pôl, when he was on his way to see the Queen. I took the opportunity to unburden my heart to him. I told him that I had secretly married a young squire who had accompanied one of the knights in his employ, and that I was grieving his loss. Philippe was shocked that the marriage had been in secret; I told him that my support for the marriage and for the birth of my child had been offered by the Duchess Valentina, who was currently providing for her care. I expressed my loyalty to the King and Queen of France, to the House of Orléans, and to himself, the Duc Philippe.

When Margaret and I were in the service of Isabeau, now

most often at l'Hôtel Barbette, the Queen sought information about Valentina, as she continued to think of her as a rival, despite her increasing control over Louis. We made sure that we told her very little; we sought to avoid intrigue, as Valentina had suffered enough.

I also saw that Bois-Bourdon was always about; he seemed to be forever awaiting some crumb of attention from Isabeau. The attention he sought rarely came, and he was both frustrated and angry.

I had just left the baby Prince Jean after nursing him one evening. I took a quiet walk down a darkened corridor, stopping in front of a window. It was a cold January night, and I just wanted a moment of respite. Suddenly, from nowhere, a strong arm encircled my waist whilst a hand covered my mouth. I was startled by Bois-Bourdon. He dragged me back into the baby's nursery where the prince was fast asleep. The under-nurse was sleeping behind the curtain in the bed that we shared. The lighted torch still gave a soft glow to the room, so that no one stumbled. This experienced courtier lay me down on the fur rug, and expertly removed all my clothing. He grabbed my breasts, sucking the precious milk from my body, relishing the nectar that belonged to the baby. I was first horrified, but then unexpectedly responded to his unwelcome caresses. I began, reluctantly to caress him in return. The wetness of my body began to flow, as he plied his fingers between my legs.

He whispered to me: 'You are a blossom, you are freshness itself. I revel in this moment. I am tired of all the ladies of this court whose responses are so devoid of feelings. But you, you say nothing but your body is responding, and you have the pure scent of summer flowers... No, I am not raping you, I am loving you..... what is your name?'

'Catharine' was all I could whisper.

'I do know that you are the young prince's wet-nurse. I dare not mention to the Queen that I have noticed you. I know her jealousy. I know how dangerous it would be for you. I know that she is capable of many means of killing, or of rendering mad. The most powerful person in the Realm, should be the King. She controls his every mood and movement. She controls also his brother and his uncle. I hate myself now, for I am the one who taught her how to manipulate all those around her.

'I promise you, Catharine, that I will not betray you.... But we must both be wary of the Queen. It is through you, that from now on, I touch a little bit of Paradise.... I had only lust in my life before.... '

===================

I could not tell what time had passed. Bois had left me. But my body, having been all aglow, was suddenly feeling only a cold shiver.

I threw my clothes on a stool; I grabbed the jug that stood on the bedside table. I was so thirsty that I emptied its contents. Then I forced myself into the bed with the under-nurse. I moved near to her so that her warm body would heat me. She woke momentarily, and put her arms around me. In her dream she called out the name of a boy.

I could not sleep... what had happened? Had the events I remembered really transpired, or had I only dreamt that my body had been ravished. I felt embarrassed but I longed for more. My body ached with yearning and exhaustion. This love would be a burden; this was not the tender love-making of my gentle husband. Bois-Bourdon loved me with the ferocity of a beast; he inflicted me with an addiction for his passion. He could never replace the holy loving of Robert. His had been pure caring and gentle comfort; Bois-Bourdon was only lustful temptation and sexuality. My Cathar feeling was that Robert was my angel, and Bois was my devil. I was torn by the excitement of them both.

I told myself that I should rest now; my path would become clear with the light of dawn.

=====================

But it did not.

The next morning the demands of my little Princeling were my reality. I bathed him with rosewater and rubbed his body with oil of lavender, I comforted him, and I gave him my breast. The under-nurse brought me breakfast; I was always hungry when I was nursing a little one. Everything was as expected.

Had anything really happened?

I carried Prince Jean to Queen Isabeau in her bedchamber, as was my custom. She was already surrounded by her most intimate courtiers and courtesans. I curtseyed and presented the baby. She raised her bejewelled hand and touched the child's cheek. She dismissed us.

I looked up and saw the face of my violator, my ravisher, my rapist, for whom my body continued to lust. I knew at that moment that the episode of the night before was real.

I took my leave from the Queen's chambers with haste, hoping that the Queen had not noticed the blush on my cheeks.

====================

I found my way to the little chapel, where I normally went to pray. My knees trembled, and I fell onto them. My rosary was in my hands, and my fingers moved nervously along the beads as I prayed. I prayed the 'Our Father' nine times and begged for His guidance. My tears washed my hands.

It was not long before Margaret entered the chapel. She saw my face and knew that something had gone terribly wrong. She knelt beside me and also prayed the 'Our Father' nine times. She put her arm around me, and drew me to her. 'Catharine, you are sobbing,' she said. 'Why do your tears flow?'

I told Margaret what had happened, every detail. I felt her grip on my shoulders getting stronger, as if to give me an anchor to centre me. 'Do not reproach yourself, you are not at fault. You are the epitome of all that is forbidden. And your response is natural; you are young and you have been alone for a long time. Do not condemn yourself.'

I felt that Margaret had offered me the absolution I needed and the confidence I required to continue. But I was still upset. I wondered how I would cope the next time Bois-Bourdon crossed my path. I did not know my feelings.... I did not know what I might do... he was irresistible.... he was temptation itself.

But I had one bizarre thought: Isabeau and I had shared seduction with the same man.

======================

I went through the chores of the day, completing every task with better than normal precision, clinging to the time-table of my life. I dared not think about the events of the previous night; I could not allow my thoughts to wander to that. I was torn between desire and despair. I still felt embarrassed.

My tasks completed, I went to my bed. I had my lighted candle on my nightstand. Before settling in, I drank heavily from the large flask of spring water that awaited me there. Then I nestled down under the covers, next to my under-nurse. I was exhausted, more by the emotional stress than by my duties ... I easily fell asleep.

I was in the twilight of my sleep when I felt hands creep under my blanket and caress my body. I was unsure – was I dreaming, or was he really here? But the touching grew more persistent and I could not roll over and ignore it.. .. Bois had returned to love me. I awoke from my sleep and he lifted me out of my bed, again onto the bear rug in front of the dying fire. There he took me, but this time with love, more than with lust. He murmured softly to me, 'You are the Queen of my heart, I had not expected to feel this way, but I do.' I was frightened because I knew that Isabeau had no limits to her treachery. If she had any doubts about the loyalty of her favourite courtier, that implicated me, I knew that my life would end quickly. Bois-Bourdon was also well aware of her capacity for evil, and promised silence and protection.

From that moment, there were unexpected pleasantries that

appeared in my life. Small gifts and even a small treasure chest filled with money and jewels found their way into my possession. He offered a small dowry for my daughter, and suggested that I move away from the palace. But that I could not do: I had my commitments here, nurturing babies was a very important and honoured task. Besides, I was still able to go to Valentina, the safest place of all.

So my life continued, I walked a dangerous tightrope. One wrong step could condemn me to the most horrific death.

I prayed constantly, both for my safety and for that of my child, and for all those who had meaning in my life, including even Bois-Bourdon, who had given me his love and commitment in the most unexpected way. I was awed by his ability to play so many roles concurrently.

BOOK VII

Charles VI

Observations of an Anonymous Chronicler

Chapter XVIII

Charles VI

-- *The Madness and the Schism* --

*'I am forgotten as a dead man out of a mind:
I am like a broken vessel.'*[30]

Forever in the mind of King Charles VI was his father's admonition to make every effort to heal the Schism that continued to divide the Church. Charles V was certain that the true Pope was the one in Avignon; Charles VI believed also in this legacy.

Charles went from time to time on expeditions to Avignon, supporting the Pope there with his finances and his forces. He desperately wanted to see the Avignon Pope as the one to unify the Church. When Clement VII died in 1394, Charles was enjoying a sane and competent moment, and took an active role.

He gathered his counsellors to decide whether a papal election should be undertaken to fill the Avignon vacancy. One of the cardinals, Pedro de Luna, had been campaigning throughout the realm, for this position even before Clement had died, based on his promise to abdicate in due course, from a position of strength. In theory, then both the Urbanist Pope

---
[30] Psalm 32:12

Boniface in Rome and the Clementine Pope could resign at the same time, allowing for the election of one Pope for all by half Clementine and half Urbanist cardinals.

In the end, Pedro de Luna was elected, and called himself Benedict XIII. It was just after this election that the decision was given to Charles VI for his agreement and confirmation. He agreed to support this election.

Benedict XIII did not do as promised; he refused to abdicate. After much unsuccessful negotiation, Charles determined to withdraw France from obedience to him.

In 1398 Charles invited the Monarch of Germany and King Wencelaus of Bohemia and King Sigismund of Hungary to a secret Lenten meeting to take a decision about the papacy. This sumptuous festivity was hosted in Rheims. Tables were laid with bright golden plates and forty course meals were served; wine flowed freely. All was provided for by Louis, Duc d'Orléans. Plied with extreme amounts of alcohol and feasting, the Heads of State were unable to take a resolution.

As promised, it was proposed that both Benedict XIII and Boniface IX resign at the same time, and a single election be held. Neither of the Popes would agree to resign. King Charles was desperate for a solution: not finding one spurred him into another attack of frenzy, from which he did not emerge for a very long time. He retired to l'Hôtel St-Pôl.

His depression was very deep. As Valentina had previously been accused of sorcery, she could not come to his aid. Suspicions about Queen Isabeau were always near the surface; she knew that an alternative solution was required.

Odette de Champdivert was the solution. She was the daughter of the chief of the Royal Stables. Bois-Boudon introduced her to Isabeau, and she agreed that she would be a suitable carer for the King. Odette was gentle and quiet, loving and compliant. Isabeau advised her about her husband's sexual appetites, hoping that Odette would exhaust him. Charles, instead, responded well to Odette, and was pleased to have her kind attention. Odette felt tender pity for her

Sovereign, and began to attend to all his needs. She took care of his personal hygiene and feeding. She bathed and perfumed his body. He revelled in her caresses. He was calmer. His only thought was to be with her. The Court called her 'La Petite Reine.'

She distracted him with a game from the Orient, with illustrated cards and symbols. The cards included a King, and Queen, a Knight, and Valet, and cards numbered 1 to 10, in four suits. The Spade was the Superior suit, the Heart was the Emotional one, the Club was the Material one, and the Diamond was the suit of Movement. Odette devised all sorts of games with these cards. She used the cards to tell him his fortune. She occupied his days in this way. His prize for winning was for her to be with him in his bed; Odette made sure that she often lost. Initially she did so to comply with Isabeau's orders; eventually she learnt to love him. Happiness reigned in his heart. That relationship produced two daughters[31].

==================

Queen Isabeau stayed at l'Hôtel Barbette which had been given to her by Louis, Duc d'Orléans. He openly resided there with her. They had no real love for each other, only lust and the desire for ultimate power. Their conspiracy was strengthened through lethal thoughts, lying words and unlawful deeds.

==================

The King's subjects, one and all, knew in their hearts, that the King's illness was not of Nature's making. He remained their *'Bien Aimé.'*

Whose hand was it that periodically dispensed the few drops of poison into his beverage?

---

[31] one of these daughters was later given a royal title, see Appendix

Chapter XIX

Conflict between Jean sans Peur And Louis d'Orléans

- 1399 – 1405 -

*'Help, O Lord; for good men have vanished;
Truth has gone from the sons of men.
Falsehood they speak one to another
With lying lips, with a false heart.'*[32]

After the passing of Charles V (in 1380), Philippe le Hardi, Duc de Bourgogne, was one of the Regents called upon to look after France until Charles VI was able to officially rule. His love of power and his personal ambitions, were legendary. This competition between la Bourgogne and the throne continued into the next generation.

The tragic royal princess Isabelle de France, Queen of England and daughter of Charles VI, had just been returned to France at the age of twelve years in 1399, two years after the death of her husband King Richard II of England. Isabelle was returned without her dowry or her jewels, in deplorable circumstances. King Henry IV, who had in fact usurped the throne of King Richard, succeeded him. He then sought to marry Richard's widow, but she would not have him, as she

---

[32] Psalm 12

was still distraught by the death of her kind husband. Further, France also opposed this marriage, due to Henry's misdeeds. Instead Henry married Joan, the widow of the Duc de Bretagne, hoping to thus acquire la Bretagne. Philippe le Hardi was angered, because as Joan's maternal uncle he would normally have had control over her activities, but as Queen of England, he would lose that power. He demanded that she appoint him as regent over her lands, so that she could only have income from them, the income that rightly belonged to her from her first husband. Philippe then allowed her to become the Queen of England, and he became guardian of her four young sons who had to remain in Bretagne. Louis, duc d'Orléans, was greatly angered, both by the treatment of Isabelle and by his inability to profit from it, whilst his rival Philippe did.

By 1399, Louis d'Orléans had so well engaged himself with Isabeau that he was able to spend not only the money that he took from Valentina, but also participated in bankrupting France's coffers. Louis' behaviour was flagrant. In his brother's name, he imposed further taxes on the people to support his extravagant appetites. His taxes reached all levels. The people were overburdened; they still suffered from a severe lack of economic activity, as well as the ravages of the Black Death: they were stunned and unable to pay. The clergy refused to pay. The house of Bourgogne was happy to hear of this plight; they became the Champions of all.

Philippe was enraged by Louis' irresponsible actions. He declared that the taxes should be practically eliminated. He sought to improve relations with England. Philippe le Hardi went further to cement his official relationship with Charles VI and Isabeau, by offering his small daughter Marguerite to be betrothed to Louis, duc de Guyene.

Louis continued to speak for his brother Charles VI, using Isabeau's authority. He stuck to his requirement that the new taxes be paid; he threatened the most dire consequences on those who could not or would not pay, despite the protestations of Philippe le Hardi. The impoverished population were required to bring their possessions to the Keep of the Louvre. Once this bounty had been collected, it was carried to the residence of the Queen where it was precisely divided in two parts. Half went to Louis and half went to Isabeau. Louis' position was thus strengthened financially, although his popularity was drastically diminished.

Isabeau, however, prudently and hypocritically, also maintained reasonable relations with Philippe le Hardi. She jealously guarded her position as Regent (without the official title until 1403), acting on her husband's authority for her own purposes.

Louis further armed himself and proposed that France step up warring against England, thinking that all would rally around the call to arms against the old enemy. He proposed that Pope Benedict XIII make a pilgrimage to Rome, to directly challenge Boniface IX. He dreamt that he might accompany the French Pope on this mission to end the Schism, and entertained the hope that he himself could be crowned Emperor of Rome.

Shortly after these conflicting relations were clearly manifest, Louis' position was enhanced by happenstance: Philippe le Hardi died suddenly and unexpectedly on the 27th April 1404. The cause of his death was officially some manner of pestilence. Prior to his demise, Philippe had ensured that his heirs would be irrevocably entwined with the ruling house of Valois.[33]

======================

Philippe's legacy went to his son, Jean sans Peur, who became the new Duc de Bourgogne. He had distinguished himself in battle, and thereby gained his appellation. He lacked his father's noble qualities. He was ageless at the age of 34. He was of small stature with no elegance. His movements were

---

[33] He betrothed his granddaughter Marguerite, (daughter of Jean sans Peur) to Louis, Duc du Guyenne. He betrothed his grandson Philippe le Bon (son of Jean sans Peur) to Michelle de France.

graceless. His head was massive; his features coarse, his manners crude and cruel. His eyes glistened with malice; he was unscrupulous. He was distrustful of all, he himself unworthy of any trust. He was faithless and merciless. He had a sly intelligence. He was ambitious and power hungry; any means to his ends were acceptable. He befriended men with the purpose of using them. He was a patient man and dangerous.

Orléans[34] had hardly a moment to relish his new found power when this new, formidable rival appeared.

---

[34] Louis d'Orléans managed to get his son Charles betrothed to Isabelle de France, former Queen of England.

BOOK VIII

Catharine and Margaret:

The Perpetual Partnership

Chapter XX

Catharine and Margaret

Royal Births

- 1401 – 1404 -

*'Fret not thyself because of evil doers,
Neither be thou envious against the workers of iniquity
For they shall soon be cut down as the grass,
And wither as the green herb.[35]'*

Isabeau continued to reside at l'Hôtel Barbette, most often in the company of Louis. Her visits to her husband at St-Pôl were rare, and undertaken with purpose. She would check on his happiness with Odette Champdivert, and pretend to visit for conjugal reasons.

Margaret and I were closely involved with Queen Isabeau's daily life, and that meant that we were with her throughout her later pregnancies, checking her physical progress as her confinements approached, and of course caring for her babies.

We were also summoned to l'Hôtel St-Pôl to deliver the two daughters of Odette, fathered by King Charles VI. I nursed these children briefly, until another wet-nurse could be

---
[35] Psalm 37

dedicated to these infants. Charles seemed overjoyed at their arrival, and played with these daughters as they grew.

Isabeau maintained her lifestyle at Court, wilfully seducing whatever courtier took her fancy. She kept Bois-Bourdon in her stable of lovers. She had an extraordinary ability to mesmerise her prey; men easily fell under her powerful spell. But her foremost companion was Louis, with whom she shared many extravagant pleasures. They jointly acquired jewels, perfumes, and luxurious fabrics; they dined on the finest foods and drank the best wine. But their sexual partnership was scandalous, even as measured by the accepted debaucheries at Court.

This really saddened me because I loved Valentina, but there was nothing I could do, I had my own vulnerability because of my furtive liaison with Bois-Bourdon.

It was 1401 when we were called upon to support Isabeau's next delivery. Once again we were summoned to Isabeau's bedchamber. The hour was early; it was a cold autumn day in October. When we arrived, we had to re-stoke the fire, as the embers from the night before were dying.

There were two of her favourite courtesans with her, but Isabeau quickly tired of their company and dismissed them. She kept calling for Louis, but he did not come. She kept just Margaret and me with her, and also two very quiet servants. She sent one of them to search for Louis; she demanded his presence. A messenger came back with the message that the Duc could not be found. (He was actually busy with another woman, as the Queen was indisposed.) She was angered by this response, as she knew that the child that was about to arrive, was his. She suspected his whereabouts.

She pushed, as by now she had become quite expert at birthing. The child appeared very quickly between the Queen's large thighs; Margaret caught the baby girl instantly. Margaret wiped her clean, and with a sharp knife cut the umbilical cord. She bound her with clean cloths, and left me to collect the afterbirth, which by now was routine for me.

The Queen suddenly looked at me. 'What is your name?'

'Catharine,' I replied. 'Then this child shall also be called Catherine,[36]' she said. These were the first kind words I ever heard Isabeau utter to a servant.

Margaret gave the Queen a brew of herbs, with a touch of Mandrake to ease the pain of birth and give her a chance to sleep. This was her tenth delivery, and her body was showing the signs of fatigue. We left her in the care of her servants, and took the new baby with us.

As always we baptised the child in secret and took her to the nursery.

==================

La Comtesse de Cani, Mariette d'Enghien and Louis d'Orléans were conducting an energetic and passionate affair, begun sometime before Isabeau had started this confinement. Louis was at least as successful as a seducer of women as Isabeau was as a seducer of men.

Louis was faithful only to himself and his ambition. He was fortunate to have both a wife, Valentina, and a mistress, Mariette, who truly loved him. His mistress, the Queen, always had her own dark scheme.

Mariette gave birth to Louis' son in Paris on the 23rd November 1402. This son was Jehan, Comte de Dunois, the famous Bastard of Orléans.[37]

=================

From the moment Isabeau had recovered from the birth of Catherine in 1401, she returned to her wanton behaviour,

---

[36] married Henry V of England, arranged by Isabeau in the Treaty of Troyes, to position him to be King of both England and France, in the event of the death of Charles VI preceding his own. This effect took away the birthright of the Dauphin of France.

[37] Dunois was brought up initially by a governess at Beauté-sur-Marne. Until the age of 10 he was reared with his (official cousin/ real half-brother) the dauphin Charles, after which Charles stayed with Yolande

feasting and fornicating with vigour, most obviously with Louis, but perhaps with many others. Bois, who still succeeded in snatching odd moments with me, had become repulsed by the Queen. He told me that Isabeau was no longer sexually fragrant, that she had lost her ability to allure and entice; her scent had deteriorated to that of a harlot.

When Louis made himself unavailable to her, she insisted on the attention of Bois-Bourdon, who carefully played his role, without any love. If none of her customary lovers were available, she would take her ladies in waiting, and dress up with them as *filles de joie*, soliciting in the very streets of Paris. She approached the nadir of life, with arrogance.

At the end of January 1403, Margaret and I were again summoned, as the Queen was beginning her confinement for what was to be her penultimate pregnancy. Although she spent most of her time at l'Hôtel Barbette, she was obliged to deliver her babies where the King resided, at l'Hôtel St-Pôl. Isabeau was unfit to deliver a child at this time; she had indulged in all manner of potions and stimulants to increase her sexual response with her various lovers. She felt that she required constant sexual activity to put the finishing touches on the features of any unborn child. Her moods oscillated from an agitated state to a sombre one. Her appearance had also changed; she looked old and bloated, and her face was flushed.

When Margaret and I arrived we took charge of her diet and daily diary. We restricted her drinking to *tizanes*[38]; we gave her bland food to eat; and we forced her to rest. We were fearful that without this regimen, the life of the new royal child, or the Queen, might be at risk. Isabeau was enraged by the limits we set. Fortunately, Margaret had the power to persuade the Queen to obey, convincing her of the dire consequences to the monarchy and to her own person, if anything should go awry.

As soon as Isabeau's behaviour quietened, her waters broke, and a tiny infant emerged from her bloated body. He was shrivelled and ugly; jaundiced and undernourished. I took

---
[38] herbal teas

him quickly into the next room and baptised him Charles, the name that Isabeau had chosen. I baptised him nearly in desperation and worry. I immediately placed him at my breast. He was so hungry that he sucked me dry. It was going to take more than my milk to bring him health, after having been carried in that unwelcoming womb.

Just as I finished this first feeding, I felt the touch of strong hands on my shoulders. It was Bois-Bourdon. 'This child is not mine, my Catharine; you can surely see that,' he said. 'He looks like a dried-up caricature of Louis d'Orléans...'

Officially this birth was shrouded in mystery. It was fortunate that there was already a Dauphin, and we did not have to bother so much about the legitimacy of this child.

======================

Margaret stayed on and spoke seriously to Isabeau. 'You must rest now; your body is exhausted. You must not become pregnant again until you are fully healed. The outcome cannot be favourable; neither to you, nor to any child you would bear. I shall devise a method of contraception for you, but you must not divulge it, or we will both be condemned by the Church.'

She made a device of linen covered with bees' wax, to be inserted into the Queen's uterus, when she anticipated sexual activity. Margaret promised to be available to help her. She prepared an herbal remedy of potentized rosemary, balsam, and parsley to be used as a douche, through a funnel of vellum. She also gave her a daily drink of medicinal wine, containing a very small amount of white lead. She emphasised the necessity of strict control so that the Queen could recover to lead a reasonably healthy life.

Because of this care, Isabeau did not become pregnant for quite some time.

Chapter XXI

Catharine and Margaret

Royal Birth

- 1407 -

'O Lord, our Lord, how excellent is Thy name in all
the earth!
who hast set thy glory above the heavens.
Out of the mouth of babes and sucklings
hast Thou ordained strength because of thine enemies
that thou mightest still the enemy and the avenger.'[39]

Margaret's collusion with Queen Isabeau was necessary; her physical health improved over the period that followed. Her behaviour modified somewhat. She did not manage to avoid pregnancy as we had hoped; she was again pregnant in 1405 but miscarried as Margaret had predicted, in the summer.

She and Louis were less flagrant in their adultery. Charles VI was still the '*Bien aimé*'; the Germanic Isabeau could never be truly accepted by the Parisians.

Isabeau declared herself to be worried about the safety of

---
[39] Psalm 8
[40] the Dauphin.

her son Louis, duc de Guyenne[40] and for that reason, organised for him to change his residence from the Palais du Louvre where Jean sans Peur was also residing. At the moment of his departure, Jean sans Peur pursued him. When he reached him he asked the young Dauphin if he wanted to return to Paris; his answer was 'yes.' Jean sans Peur was hailed as his saviour for returning him to the Palais du Louvre.

Isabeau kept trying to protect her power and therefore, sought to engineer reconciliation between Louis d'Orléans and Jean sans Peur. She realised that their continuing quarrel could result in a bloody civil war, threatening the monarchy and the country. She felt herself an unfortunate pawn in this continuing conflict between the houses of Bourgogne and Orléans. She organised a meeting[41] , and embarrassed Jean and Louis into a rapprochement: she managed to get them to embrace, take communion together, and sleep in the same bed, thus promising an improved relationship by dialogue instead of armed conflict.

Sadly the forces of competition and jealousy were stronger than any familial agreement.

=============

In 1406 there was a double wedding at Compiègne: Isabelle de France married Charles d'Orléans[42], and Jean de Touraine[43] married Jacqueline de Bavière[44]. It was an occasion for all the families to be together. Valentina attended with Louis, to see their son married. Charles VI and Isabeau attended to rejoice at the weddings of their daughter and their son. Isabeau's brother, Louis de Bavière brought other members of that family to the festivities. Jean sans Peur, with his family, was of course an honoured guest. He said he wanted only that which

---

[41] October 1405
[42] son Louis d'Orléans and Valentina
[43] officially son of Charles VI and Isabeau, in reality son of Louis d'Orléans and Isabeau. He took the title 'Touraine' which was Louis' old title (given to him by Charles V at this death)
[44] daughter of William IV de Bavière, niece of Jean sans Peur

would benefit France. The fragile peace amongst these factions was always under threat.

When Charles VI was without his Queen at St-Pôl, he would recover, and start to attempt to resume his proper role as King, frequently nearing the pronouncement of some good decision. He could not abide Isabeau's presence in his sane moments. She saw to it that he was well drugged when she visited him at St-Pôl. These visits were generally followed by Charles' periods of madness. Isabeau always managed to visit him alone, especially when she suspected herself to be pregnant. In this way she maintained her power and control.

=============

In 1407 Isabeau was again pregnant. She endured the heat of the summer and welcomed the cool autumn that followed. She stayed the whole time at her home at l'Hôtel Barbette, where she had shared many moments with Louis d'Orléans.

But she had begun to tire of Louis. His inability to usurp his brother and become King bothered her. He was still very handsome and seductive, but his endless philandering ceased to make him special to her. He had no inner strength, just the same kind of talent that she had, for manipulating others.

Nevertheless, she maintained erotic relations with him, as she was again carrying his child. The fact of her pregnancy had been kept hidden from nearly everyone.

She learnt from Bois-Bourdon, who spoke with admiration and fear, of Jean sans Peur's power, wealth and capacities for turning events to his advantage. All of these were characteristics that she admired. The confirmation of these truths, excited Isabeau. She desired his dark strength and wanted his alliance. She planned to seduce him in the near future.

She was having these thoughts although her body was tired. The frequent pregnancies and the excesses of her lifestyle had taken their toll.

On All Saints Day, Margaret and I returned from our

sojourn with Valentina at Blois, where I was able to spend some sweet moments with my nine-year old daughter. Valentina had decided that Christine Valentine would stay with her, and eventually become a lady in waiting for her daughter, Marie. I was very happy with this arrangement for the safety and education of my daughter, also for myself, as in this way I could continue to visit Valentina.

We knew that we were arriving late for Isabeau's confinement, but were pleased that her travail had not yet begun. We were desperately required, as Isabeau was unwell. We slept on small wooden cots on the floor in her bedchamber. We were grateful for the warmth of the fire and the luxury of fur blankets, as winter was approaching quickly. Even the late autumn was very cold.

At dusk, on the 6th November, Isabeau's labour pains commenced. A few hours later Louis arrived, and stood hidden behind the bed curtains, at the head of her bed. Isabeau screamed with pain at about midnight; about two hours later, her child arrived, sliding easily into life. Margaret washed the Queen and I washed her baby girl. She was beautiful and sturdy; she resembled Louis, but in sharp contrast to the shrivelled baby Charles. After she was swaddled, I began to carry her out of the room. At that moment Louis emerged from the darkness and looked at her and at Isabeau. He kissed Isabeau on the cheek. He followed me out of the room, and spoke to me. 'Take this child away with you; there is a carriage outside. My wife Valentina is in it and she awaits you.' I had barely time to gather the placenta and prepare it, and to offer prayers. I baptised her 'Jehanne, fille de la Reine.'

Under the Queen's bed there stood a small white coffin, already inscribed with the name 'Philippe'. It was needed so that the public could be told that the Queen had miscarried, whether or not that was the case. There had been fear that any child, in particular a male heir to the throne, could be kidnapped by any one of the competing factions, so a different public reality was required. Even the unstable vindictive Queen could not know.

Some stones were placed in the tiny coffin, and the Queen was told that her child was born dead. The little coffin was later removed. Margaret stayed with her, much dismayed that she had to take part in this deception.

Louis stayed on with Isabeau, doing his utmost to comfort her; she was unaccustomed to his attentive devotion. She expressed regret at the loss of their child, and allowed herself the excuse of the birth to repel his prompt sexual advances.

They shared supper together most evenings, but she would often retire early, begging fatigue.

================

Her thoughts were firmly focused on Jean sans Peur. She encouraged Louis to invite him to another meeting, in the interest of their continuing reconciliation.

On the 14th November, at Louis' invitation, Jean sans Peur arrived at l'Hôtel Barbette to further these negotiations. Jean sans Peur was escorted into Louis' study where portraits of Louis' lovers were hung on the wall. The first portrait that Jean noticed was that of his own wife, Marguerite de Hainaut. He was shocked, but composed himself, and exited, indicating a priority elsewhere. He begged Louis' forgiveness for his abrupt departure.

Minutes later, Jean sans Peur arrived at the Queen's apartments, in a most agitated state. 'Isabeau, *ma Reine*, I come to you directly. I see now that you and I must unite. In compliance with your wishes, I have just been to meet with Louis and was escorted into his study where are hung the portraits of his many mistresses. I want you to know that you have a rival for his love; your rival is my wife. Her portrait hangs boldly there.'

Isabeau was both shocked and furious. She had always known that Louis has been a philanderer, but always trusted that he exercised some discretion in his conquests.

'Madame, I know now that I love you, with uncontrollable passion; it is not just anger that I feel, but a true kinship with you. We have been wronged by the same man. We now have a common cause. I give you my homage, I kneel at your feet. Pronounce your word, Isabeau, I shall serve you to eliminate Louis. It must be done in secret and with great stealth; we know that the King loves his brother very much. But, if you do not support me, I shall become your enemy.' Jean sans Peur had taken control.

Isabeau responded, 'we are fortunate to be comforted by each other....' She led him to her bedchamber to seal the bargain they had made. 'Be gentle with me, my Jean, you know that I recently lost his child... let it be your seed that eventually takes the Crown.'

==================

Queen Isabeau organised a dinner for Wednesday, the 23rd November at l'Hôtel Barbette, for Louis d'Orléans. During the course of the evening, Isabeau asked Louis about the progress of the reconciliation with Jean sans Peur. She asked, 'how can you be sure that he is sincere?.... you cannot trust him. He is false and hard. He has no scruples. He is undoubtedly jealous of you, in every way. You are handsome and charming; he is ugly and gauche. He must have been affected in some way when he saw the portrait of Marguerite de Hainaut, his wife....I must admit that knowing about that made me jealous as well... I do not understand how you have any room in your heart for anyone but me. I do understand your passions, you and I are kindred spirits...but still...'

Louis begged Isabeau's forgiveness for being so thoughtless with Jean sans Peur. He promised to be as caring with her as he had been since the very recent 'still birth'... 'I know you suffer, dear Isabeau, I shall continue to love you gently...'

Suddenly, their amorous moment was shattered by a disturbance in the next room. The King's valet, Thomas de Courteheuse, rushed in to interrupt them. He said that he came urgently from the King. 'I bear a message from your brother, the King. He requires your presence, directly. There are matters of great importance to both of you, which must be discussed forthwith.'

'*Bien sûr*, I come without delay. Forgive me, dear Isabeau, but ... the affairs of State.......'

Isabeau answered, 'Of course, my beloved, my thoughts will follow you every step of the way.' Louis did not detect her real intentions which differed from her words.

Louis took his leave in all haste. He mounted his mule, taking only two valets, his squire Jacob, and two horsemen hurriedly mounted onto the same horse, with him for support, and to bear torches to light his way.

Assassins were staying in the house opposite l'Hôtel Barbette which Jean sans Peur had acquired some time previously. They appeared to be brigands; this evening they had positioned themselves along the wall just at the entrance of the alley, near rue Blancs-Manteaux.

They saw Louis appear, easily visible by the light of the torch that his valet held. They quickly encircled him, intent on the attack. One of the assassins cruelly severed his left hand using a curved hatchet. Louis was barely able to maintain his hold on his mule with his right. Then his right hand was severed, to stop it from raising the devil.

'I am the Duc d'Orléans!' he shouted, thinking that his attackers would flee when they knew who he was.

'He is the one we seek!' they retorted. They answered with more blows, one cutting him from ear to ear. The next one cracked his skull. As he was about to fully succumb, Jean sans Peur appeared, and came upon him to deliver the final blow. He then took a torch and put it close to Louis' face to assess for himself that he was really dead. He assured himself that it was so.

During the brutal assault, the horse bearing the two horsemen galloped away in fright. Louis' beloved squire Jacob expired with him. One of the valets ran away.

The other valet returned to l'Hôtel Barbette to reveal to Isabeau the criminal incident that he had just witnessed. Upon receiving this news, Isabeau was suitably overcome. She went pale and fainted dead away. Her servants immediately saw to her condition, and she was carried swiftly to l'Hôtel St-Pôl. Margaret accompanied her.

====================

Bois-Bourdon was Isabeau's first visitor in her apartments at l'Hôtel St-Pôl, on the very night of her arrival there. She was grateful for his company. 'Are you certain, my Bois, that Louis is dead?' she asked.

'Yes, my Queen, I can confirm it. I saw his corpse being lifted, covered in blood. Both his hands had been severed from his body. His skull was cracked, his brain was oozing from his head. It was most brutal..... His remains were placed in the house of le Maréchal de Rieux. '

'It was a necessary death, Bourdon. You must keep this information to yourself; I charge you to prevent any suspicion of my complicity in this affair. I further charge you to stay close to the Duc de Bourgogne, dearest Friend. We need his protection. He is powerful and ruthless. He is without remorse.

'I have already mentioned you to him. He will remunerate you well for your efforts.

'But first, you must go to Blois and inform my dear sister-in-law of her loss, and extend my deepest affection to her. We all share her sorrow, and pray for her safe journey to Paris.'

==================

At the funeral Mass for Louis, there were many mourners. Jean sans Peur wept with great sadness as did the other princes.

The provost of Paris initiated an intense investigation of the crime.

Jean sans Peur confessed to the Duc de Berri and the King of Sicily that he had been tempted by the devil himself to commit this despicable homicide. He asked their forgiveness.

He then rode with all speed to Flanders. One hundred twenty cavaliers from the house of Orléans were in pursuit, but did not manage to seize him. He was welcomed in Lille where the Church declared him the saviour of King Charles VI, as it was commonly thought that Louis was planning to usurp his brother. By this time, Louis had become truly an unpopular royal, both with the Parisians because of his greed, and with the Church for his lack of morality, and also with the administration of the powerful Université de Paris because of his politics.

======================

The Queen despatched Bois-Bourdon to Flanders to promise Jean sans Peur her undying support.

Chapter XXII

Catharine and Valentina

At Blois

- 1407- 1408 -

*'In the Lord put I my trust:
How say ye to my soul,
Flee as a bird to your mountain?'*[45]

I felt frightened that I was carrying this new princess, my Jehanne, in my arms, escaping from l'Hôtel Barbette. It took me a moment to notice Valentina's covered carriage, as she was in an ordinary one, not a royal one. She had no obvious entourage, but was accompanying a group of travelling merchants, probably from Italy. When I saw Valentina, I noticed that she was plainly dressed; her face was covered by a heavy veil.

I quickly entered her carriage, and we were off. As it was the middle of the night we were unable to go far. In a matter of minutes we were delivered to a safe house, nearby. We were ushered into the kitchen where we were warmed by the fire and given a cup of wine each. I also asked for water, as this baby had a voracious appetite, and I had to replenish myself. We

---
[45] Psalm 11

were not given a room, as we would depart as soon as daylight broke.

Valentina gazed at the child with tenderness. She could see her husband's features in this infant's face. She was gentle and loving and kind with Jehanne; she exhibited her great capacity for caring. She whispered to me, 'this child belongs to the house of Orléans; she will be unknown to the Crown, but protected as the precious seed of Louis because of the ancient prophecy[46].' Apart from those few words, she said very little, she understood the danger of the enterprise in which we were now engaged.

She told me about another of Louis' natural children, a little boy of five years, called Jehan. Valentina had taken great delight in her many encounters with him. He was being brought up as one of her own in the Blois nursery, alternating with his lengthy stays with Charles, the eventual Dauphin.

The dawn came quickly, and we packed ourselves into the comfortable warmth of the carriage. We travelled south towards the Loire. We made several stops at friendly houses, convents, and hospices, all under the authority of the Orléans family. This kind of secret travel was familiar to me; I adapted quickly. Despite the sodden ground that always appeared by midday, we made good progress. It was the only moment when I actually hoped for the cold, so that our path would be passable. We were fortunate that there were Orléans soldiers accompanying our convoy, so that we could feel safe. It took us about a week to reach the gates of the Château Blois.

As it was Valentina's home, we were welcomed with special warmth. The first to reach us were Valentina's daughter and mine. Marie and Christine Valentine ran towards us joyously, hand in hand. There was endless chatter; they had to tell us all that they had been doing. They showed us their needlework and their calligraphy. They sang their songs in harmony. Their abundant energy was contagious. I was pleased to see how Christine Valentine was flourishing here. Valentina had seen to

---

[46] 'The Crown of France could be lost by the Treachery of a Whore, but saved by a Virgin...' the Monk Bede, 7th Century

it that she was beautifully dressed; life with Valentina had given her a natural highborn bearing. My daughter was like a little princess; I nearly felt that I should curtsey to her.

Valentina told me that Christine Valentine's warm nature had given Marie the companionship that she really needed; their relationship had given Marie a stronger and more outgoing presence. I was grateful for the love and the laughter they shared, as I could not be there to give my daughter the love she needed.

The little girls had many questions for us. But the most important one was about the baby in my arms. They wanted to know who she was. 'Is she ours?' Marie asked. 'Is she my sister?' asked Christine Valentine.

'She is ours now,' I answered. 'Her mother died, and I am looking after her,' I lied. 'She has been placed in my care; she is fragile now, after the winter journey we have just endured. But later, if you wish, you may spend some time with her. Her name is Jehanne.'

Our accommodations in Blois were comfortable, albeit small. The heavy curtains insulated us from the cold. The fire gave us good warmth. I had a small cot for Jehanne. My bed was large enough so that Christine Valentine could stay the night with me when she wished.

We settled into a gentle routine. I had no difficult tasks to perform; Valentina kept a staff of servants around me. My only assignment was to nurse and nurture my small charge. The girls were spellbound by my stories.

Valentina paid me visits as often as her obligations allowed. Her gentle but powerful presence comforted me. Being in her household gave me a feeling of security. There were no threats here; there were no thoughts of Queen Isabeau or of Louis or of Jean sans Peur, or of the corrupt court, or even of Bois-Bourdon.

One evening, just a few days after we had arrived, she came into my apartment. There was a look of sadness on her face. Her beautiful blue eyes were filled with tears. 'I feel a terrible sense of foreboding. Catharine, I do not know where it is from, but it is in the cards when I read them, and in the sound of the loud, shrill cry of the crow. Lately that ghostly shriek has been following me like a threatening spectre. I am deeply troubled,' she lamented.

'I come here to your apartment for solace; I know that this place under my care, brings you a feeling of safety. And I come to you, to feel it also. In your company I can still feel serene. I know we share secrets that bind us together. I need your commitment to stay in my household. I will help to smooth the path you must follow, but you must care for my husband's child, whatever obligation that may involve. Please Catharine, help me, I trust you as a sister.'

I was honoured and touched by her unfailing belief in me. I always knew that I would never forsake her. I touched my rosary, and prayed my thanks to God. But I was worried; I had never seen her so distraught. Her uncanny sense of events was disturbing.

Jehanne felt it also, I am sure; she cried all that night and demanded that I hold her until the morning came. I took her to my bed; I caressed her body from the top of her tiny head to her little feet. I delineated her shape with the stroke of my hand, to make her aware of her size and her space. She was now mine.

====================

Several days later, on the 26th November, I believe, just at eventide, there was great agitation in the palace courtyard. I heard the sounds of clattering hoofs; I thought the whole army had arrived. There were screams from the unprepared staff, wondering what could possibly be amiss.

In the background, I heard the unmistakable voice of Bois-Bourdon. He was requesting to be admitted to pay respects to Madame Valentina.

As Valentina was just then in my apartments, he was escorted to her there. She sat on the foot of my bed as he entered. He bowed deeply to her, ignoring my presence. His face was drawn and tired, more stressed than I had ever seen him before. He spoke to her in a hoarse whisper, 'Your husband is dead, my Lady; he has been murdered. There is a rumour that the culprit could be the Comte de Cani[47].

'The Queen dispatched me to escort you to Paris, so that all the family may mourn together. His earthly remains now rest at L'église de Blancs-Manteaux.'

Bois-Bourdon took the liberty of allowing his eyes to rest on me and the child that I was holding. He said nothing, but there was a longing in his look.

Valentina sighed and shuddered, holding back the grief and fear that was striking her chest, making her feel winded. Her hands covered her face, she shook her head, and she moaned, '*Rien ne m'est plus – plus ne m'est rien...*'[48] She said no more.

She composed herself rose and responded to the matter at hand, 'Monsieur, thank you for advising me. You and your men must sup and rest. We will all mount and ride at dawn. I shall be accompanied at the funeral by my son the Comte d'Angoulême and my daughter-in-law Isabelle. They will follow by carriage.

Her voice began to tremble as she clenched her hands tightly to steel herself. 'Tell me, Bois-Bourdon, on which day and at what time was life stolen from the Duc d'Orléans?'

'Madame, it was on the evening of the 23rd November, after he had supped with the Queen. He understood that he was being summoned urgently by his brother, the King. He was set upon by eight unknown assassins. I viewed his lifeless body at about 9:00 o'clock.'

Tears rolled down her cheeks, but she continued speaking bravely, as if she did not even notice them. 'I thank you for your candour, and for escorting me tomorrow. I bid you good night.'

Valentina was stunned that she had experienced her feeling of deep foreboding just at the moment of Louis' death. She unclenched her hands seeing the deep marks her nails had

---

[47] husband of Mariette d'Enghien, mother of Jehan de Dunois
[48] nothing is more for me, more for me is nothing...

made in her own flesh. She gazed toward me, but seemed to be looking through me.

===================

Late that night when everyone slept, I again felt a hand on my body. Bois had returned to me. He lay beside me. I accepted him, but I could no longer trust him, and knew that this would be the last time.

Just then, Jehanne whimpered. I begged him to leave me then, as the child needed to be suckled. He left, probably also knowing that our intimacy had reached its end. Just before he departed, he cautioned me: 'There is conflict and treachery everywhere, Catharine, you must be cautious for your life, and the life of that Orléans child you nurse.'

===================

Valentina went to the Abbey at St Denis to pray for the soul of her late husband. Then she proceeded to l'Hôtel St-Pôl in Paris, rather belatedly. She petitioned her brother-in-law King Charles to find and punish Louis' murderer. Charles assured her that the provost of Paris had already been charged to make an intense investigation of the crime.

There was nothing more for Valentina to do in Paris, so she made ready to depart. Just as she was leaving, Margaret saw her and stopped her. She curtseyed and kissed her hands. She offered her condolences on the terrible loss of her husband. Valentina bade her rise and kissed her. Margaret quietly asked if she might accompany her to Blois. She begged to join the Duchess' household. 'I cannot bear it here any longer,' she said. 'The intrigues that permeate these halls frighten me, this place is a malevolent maze, a vipers' nest. I know in my heart that the Queen is the evil spirit behind your husband's death; I cannot prove it, but I do feel it. I am too terrified to remain.'

Valentina answered, 'Come, dear Margaret. I know your worth. You will accompany me now and stay with Catharine.'

====================

Peace reigned at Blois; it was lovely to have Margaret back in our lives.

We heard that on the 28th February 1408, Jean sans Peur returned to Paris. He had admitted his guilt in the murder of Louis, Duc d'Orléans, but was praised for having taken this action. It was deemed a necessary deed, to protect France and the King, from Louis' excessive taxes and from his threat to usurp the throne. Jean sans Peur was praised by the Church[49], by the Université de Paris, and by the people, and officially forgiven by the King who had been duped into signing a pardon. Jean sans Peur was of course supported by Isabeau; their political alliance was strengthened by their adultery. They met at St Denis ostensibly to pray, but instead they copulated in the abbey, on the very tomb of Louis.

Valentina was devastated by these great dishonours to her husband's memory. She had to use all her powers to prevent her father from exacting revenge, which could have caused yet greater conflict. She greatly fortified her home and her holdings.

On the 18th March, Charles came to the realisation that he had forgiven Jean sans Peur for the murder of his brother. He also realised that he had spent the night before this pardon was granted, with his wife. His memory was totally clouded, but his regret for both these actions, was genuine.

Valentina responded with a visit to Charles in September, wherein she petitioned him to reverse the pardon he had granted; he did so and the letters were nullified. Jean sans Peur was officially prevented from approaching the palaces of the King, the Queen, and the Duchess d'Orléans.

====================

---

[49] Jean Petit, a monk of the Abbey of St Denis accepted a large bribe from Jean sans Peur to gain approval from the Church for his exoneration.

In the November of that year, our beloved Valentina mysteriously passed away. I could not understand whether it had to do with her continuing grief for her faithless husband, or whether there had been an unknown hand, an agent of Isabeau, who might have administered a poison. I distrusted all but Margaret.

Sadly, turmoil[50] reigned not only in our corner of France, but throughout the country.

==================

---

[50] Civil war between the Armagnacs and the Bourguignons pervaded France.

Chapter XXIII

Catharine, Margaret and Jehanne

- 1408 – 1411 -

*'God is our refuge and our strength,
a very present help in trouble.
Therefore we will not fear,
though the earth be removed and
though the mountains be carried into the midst of
the sea.'*[51]

There was a sealed letter that Valentina had left in my possession. The cover bore the words 'to be opened in the event of my sudden departure.' Upon her death, I opened it.

I read the words:

---

[51] Psalm 46

> My dear Catharine
>
> Now that I am gone, you will no longer be safe at Blois. You and Margaret must take Jehanne away from here. You will travel with merchants, just as we did when we arrived here.
>
> Your way has been prepared. Your destination will be Domrémy in Lorraine. You will be received at the household of Jacques and Isabelle d'Arc. They will advise you from then on.
>
> My children and also your Christine Valentine will be safe; they are already known to the House of Orléans. I have appointed the duc d'Armagnac to be their guardian and protector.
>
> If I have departed this life when you read this letter, I beg you to pray for my soul, and to think well of me. Know I have done all that I could.
>
> Yours in God
> Valentina

I folded the letter and replaced it in my bosom. I gathered a few necessary belongings, including a hidden box containing gold coins and a list of safe Orléans destinations. Then I went to my daughter, and embraced her. I kissed her eyes, and her cheeks and her forehead. I prayed with her, knowing that it might be the last time we would share such a moment. I spoke no other words.

Margaret and I did as Valentina instructed, and departed with Jehanne in our care, in all deliberate haste. We retreated into the safety of the familiar underground network of the Cathar faith, which rendered us virtually invisible. We took care to maintain our anonymity; we knew that we would eventually reach Domrémy according to Valentina's instructions, but knew also that to hurry could expose us. The chaos and turmoil within France continued, and it continued to instil fear and caution within us. We moved carefully but frequently from place to place, carrying the letters of introduction that we earned at each hospice, convent, manor house, or castle that had taken us in. We also had letters of credit from Valentina, to independently assure our prosperity. We were either under the care of the various religious houses or the Orléans family, or the Visconti family, and eventually the Armagnacs.

We used our midwifery skills everywhere; we were always in demand. I particularly noticed that Margaret's skills were growing. I watched her manage some very difficult deliveries during the time we were travelling. She seemed to be able to calm mothers that I could not help. I asked her one day how she managed it. She was unaware that she had developed a sort of magnetism about her; she just called it the power of suggestion. She 'suggested' that the women be calm, and trust in her, and the most difficult were easily delivered. It was nearly a power of hypnosis. My confidence increased as we worked together.

During our wanderings, we began to share more of our thoughts and ideas. Margaret and I never feared anything of each other; we simply shared. We reached a plateau of understanding that I believe was rarely achieved between any two people. Together we embraced all the facets of understanding of birth, life, and death. Every task we undertook gave us a new experience and added to our learning. Margaret was indeed a *Parfaite*, and I followed her closely. We knew that we had a serious responsibility; we shared in rearing Jehanne. We knew that her destiny would be important, not only as our mission, but also for our beloved France.

====================

During this time, we managed to give more than the required

care to Jehanne. After I finished nursing her I got her on to solid foods, chewing for her until her teeth had grown strong enough to manage. Throughout this time, I kept my body and my diet very pure; she depended upon me for her very existence. I never nursed another child after Jehanne.

We repeated words and prayers to her; she was bright and learned rapidly. She learned to be strong in her body, from our long walks and pilgrimages. She ran ahead and found secret hiding places, from which she would leap out and surprise us. We taught her that, for the sake of safety, in particular in our travels, most often it could be important to hide oneself.

We taught her to hear God's word everywhere; we prayed in the forest, we prayed at her bedside. We prayed in chapels; we sang God's praises wherever we were, sometimes quietly, sometimes with great volume, always with enthusiasm.

We taught her the sounds of the Church bells: she learnt to distinguish the chimes of happiness from the peals that begged for care and cautioned all those in earshot.

She learnt from Nature: she learnt to listen to what she heard; she learnt to look carefully at what she saw; she learnt to feel what she touched. She became aware of every detail of her surroundings.

We taught her the 'Our Father', but called it 'Our God's Prayer' so as not to prejudice her about the 'masculinity' of God. After all, she was being carefully raised without the presence of any man. Her occasional encounters with clergy did not matter really; they prayed with us, in just the way we did.

===================

In 1407, Isabelle d'Arc had left her home, ostensibly to begin a difficult confinement at a convent some distance away. She returned in 1408 to Domrémy without her child, explaining that the child was unwell and had to be left at the convent for special care. Her sister-in-law, Jeanne d'Arc, who had 'officially' been in attendance at the birth, was named as a Godmother, and charged as a contact for delivering the child back to the d'Arc household.

====================

In late 1411 we arrived in Orléans, and were welcomed at the home of the Treasurer General Jacques Bouchet. He had been Valentina's conduit to convey funds to the Arc family in preparation for their ultimate role in the care of Jehanne.

In early 1412, we began to prepare for our journey to Domrémy. We did not expect this journey to be significantly more difficult than any of our previous ones, but the preparations that we had to make, had more to do with explaining this journey to our precocious Jehanne.

I spoke to her carefully. '*Ma petite Jehanne*, you know that we have now arrived at Orléans. We are here because our dear Valentina willed it. I know that you do not remember her, but you know from Margaret and me that she was a very important and kind person, who has given us the means to proceed.

'We will soon depart Orléans to join your mother and father in Domrémy, near Vaucouleurs, in the Meuse.'

'To my mother and father?' Jehanne replied. 'But I have been with you always… are you not my *Maman*? Is that why I call you Catharine? And what about Margaret? I always thought of her as my auntie….'

'It is true,' I answered, 'that we have been together for a long time. You were entrusted to our care, because we can protect you. We are able to move through many situations, without being memorable or visible. But do not worry, we will continue to stay with you.'

'But who are my parents then?' she asked.

'You belong to the house d'Arc. I will tell you more about who you are when you are a bit older, but for now, I only hope that you can look forward with joy to being with them in a permanent home, and with the others in your family.'

I could see the worry on her young, fair brow. Change is

always worrying for the very young. She agreed to accept this news, but she did this with her capacity for intellectual understanding. Her heart was still obstinate, and her nature was obsessive for detail.

Then I dressed her. I had to remove her brightly coloured clothes, according to the guidance given me by Jacques Bouchet. I dressed her in a simple garment, in dull colours, mostly brown and dark blue. She was startled, and felt insecure. She questioned me about this change. I told her that we were disguising ourselves. We would have to live a new role in our lives; we would now blend with the rural peasantry so as not to arouse any suspicion of our origins. I tried to make it one of our games, but she was too clever to simply accept this change as a game. I could not tell her when the charade would end.

She was concerned that without her beautiful clothing, people would not notice that she was a princess. I had to tell her that people often called her Princess because of her outstanding gentle and pious comportment and bearing, not because of her attire. But I also told her that such titles were of no importance in life, and that if indeed she were never again addressed as Princess, she should pay it no heed. We are all royal and pleasing in the eyes of God. She seemed somewhat dissatisfied with this answer, even so.

====================

It was fitting that we were to embark upon our journey in February, just as Lent began. Our dull garments were suitable to this time in the Church year.

After she thought about her changing circumstances, Jehanne began to ply us with her many questions about the journey to Domrémy. 'I suppose that I have been waiting for a long time to reach my *Maman* and *Papa*, without even knowing it,' she said. 'What are they like, Catharine? Have you seen them? Will I understand them? Do I resemble them? Do they pray as we do? Do they have a pleasant castle and a comfortable household?'

I could not honestly answer all her questions, but told her that castles were unlikely, and that the household would not be large. 'Your parents are good Catholic people. They live in their own home, right next to the Church. They will keep you safe,' I said.

A day or two later, Jacques d'Arc arrived, accompanied by his eldest son. Jacques, was a strong, healthy man, confident in his bearing. I immediately felt the wisdom of Valentina in choosing him as head of the household where Jehanne would grow and learn.

Jehanne was also pleased to meet her elder brother Pierre. She found him easy to chat to; she began to look forward to meeting her other brother. He also told her about their life at Domrémy, in particular about the farm and the animals. She began to become impatient for the journey.

======================

Jacques d'Arc, aided by his son, organised our departure. We left in a covered harvest cart pulled by two horses, escorted by some guards supplied by Jacques Bouchet.

We were cosy within this cart, as we were covered with furs; Jacques d'Arc and his son were without, holding the reins. They were dressed for this journey, wearing warm fur-lined cloaks and huge fur mittens.

The actual travel to Domrémy was strange for the little one, despite her initial enthusiasm. She would start a sentence, 'Catharine....' but then could not finish her train of thought. She seemed to notice that the expression on my face showed signs of strain and stress. It was true. I was worried about this new life to which we were moving. We held hands tightly, and I entwined my Rosary between Jehanne's little fingers. We repeated the God's Prayer and the Hail Mary in loud whispers, in time with the horses' hoofs and the creaking wheels of the cart.

Margaret was feeling uncomfortable, as the shaking of our

vehicle was harsh on her back. She was beginning to feel her years. She tried to sing her pain away. Jehanne would join her from time to time, taking breaks among the mysteries of the Rosary. I joined them also; we felt our hearts uplifted. Jacques heard our singing, and he joined in, his powerful yet dulcet tones complementing and often overtaking our own.

Our song had transformed our discomfort into harmony; we praised God for His Goodness and His Blessings.

Chapter XXIV

Jehanne at Domrémy

- 1412 -

'I will love Thee, O Lord, my strength.
The Lord is my rock, and my fortress, and my deliverer
My God, my strength, in whom I will trust...' [52]

Suddenly the horses slowed to a walk. The trail was suddenly more difficult to manage, because of the heavy snows that still lay on the ground. We looked out and saw the trees with bare branches covered with ice. We heard them crackle in the wind, but were most taken with their appearance. The thick ice sparkled in the setting sun; it was a beautiful sight to behold.

The smell of a burning fire, the curls of smoke exiting the chimneys, the sounds of animals moaning: these were the experiences that greeted us. I touched Jehanne's hand: I had a strong feeling of knowing this place; it came over me like a wave. I said, *'Ma petite*, I know this place although I have never seen it before. Do not be deceived by the simple appearance of your home; it will be a sanctuary for you and for us all.'

Jacques stopped the cart just in front of the building;

---
[52] Psalm 18

Pierre held onto the horses. Jacques rushed to the door. Jehanne's new mother appeared at the entrance with outstretched arms to greet us. She gathered my charge close to her. She kissed her and whispered a word of love. I felt a twinge in my heart. Was it jealousy?

Margaret noticed this propitious moment. Our duties towards Jehanne would be changed forever. Our role would be transparent; its importance, however, could not waver. We would have to teach our princess to become a peasant.

====================

We entered the large hall. The room was warm and welcoming. There was a large trestle table covered with a white cloth and lit by stubby candles. There were various sheep cheeses, fresh crusty rye bread, and slices of salt pork. There were large pitchers of milk and of wine on the table.

We were grateful for this repast. Jehanne, however, was so tired, both from the journey and from the many changes with which she was striving to cope, that she contented herself with just a small crust of bread and a tumbler of milk. She was falling asleep as she ate. Jacques was aware, and carried her directly upstairs to her wooden cot. He was proud to take her there; he had made it for her. It was lined with lambs' skin and had a warm woven wool blanket on it, that Isabelle d'Arc had made. He gently placed her tired little body where it belonged.

I followed him up to make sure that she was asleep. A candle was glowing in a corner of the room; above it was a simple wooden cross, without the body of Christ on it.

I noticed that the room, although small, was beautifully clean, with whitewashed walls. There were rods round the room for hanging our clothing. The smells of dried lavender and rushes pervaded the quarters. Apart from the cot, there were two more narrow beds, to accommodate Margaret and me. They each had goose down filled mattresses and pillows, sheets of linen, and blankets of wool.

I followed Jacques down the stairs. We all held hands for

our evening prayers. We blessed each other, we kissed each other, and we thanked each other for the joyous outcome of this day. Jacques put a big log on the fire and banked it with the cinders. We blew out all the candles, save one, and climbed the stairs.

Jacques checked the animals; Isabelle came with us to look in on her new daughter. The Arc boys went quietly to their beds, and Margaret and I went to ours.

====================

Margaret and I had new roles; we would be known as 'distant cousins'. We would become the midwives of the district. Secretly we would tutor Jehanne, as she had much to learn about her new reality.

We would be the guardians of her truth.

====================

The next morning we were awakened by the Bells. The Church was very close to the d'Arc home. Jehanne opened her eyes and looked at me, yawning. 'Catharine, I have slept so well, but, where are we?' I answered her: 'Jehanne we reached your family yesterday, you are now in your home. Your parents are Jacques and Isabelle d'Arc. You will live a peasant and a pleasant life here.'

'Can we pray now, Catharine?' 'Of course, Jehanne.' I knelt beside her cot and began to recite the God's prayer. She joined in. When we had finished, she said, 'I want to talk secretly to God now, but I want you to listen also. God bless all those who love me, and those who do not. I pray that I should understand them.'

At that moment I realised that this little child had composed her own prayer. I gazed at her and was amazed at the person I saw. Even though she now had to live as a peasant, her genuine fine heredity was evident. Her beauty was the legacy of her natural father; her charm she had inherited from her royal mother. Her goodness had come from Valentina's nurturing nature; her strength had come from my milk.

We dressed quickly in warm clothing and descended the stairs. There were bowls of water and soap for each of us, near the fire. We washed our faces and hands.

Isabelle went directly to Jehanne and spoke to her. 'Dear Jehanne, what can I offer you for breakfast? I know that you must be hungry; you ate so little last evening. I will help you. I will show you about. You will go to the Church with Catharine, Margaret, and me; I will introduce you to the Priest, and he will hear your prayers.'

Jehanne felt the love in her voice, and responded positively. She looked at her mother, and noticed her dark hair escaping from her bonnet. She could not help but return the beaming smile that Isabelle gave her. Her face was radiant: she was delighted at last, to have a little girl. Isabelle continued, 'later, you can watch me turn wool into yarn on my spinning wheel. One day you will be able to do it yourself, and weave on our loom, too. But you needn't worry about this now, my darling; at this moment the only thing you have to do is to pray diligently and to have kind thoughts about all those who surround you, and to play. By playing you will learn all the joys that the countryside can offer you.

'Your brothers will show you the animals; you may help with their feeding if you wish. There is not so much to do with the animals at this time of year; in the spring, you can go with them into the fields. You will find that our lives are busy, but you will settle in soon enough, and it will be just fine.

'I am happy that we have Catharine and Margaret here. They are here for you and will continue to teach you many things that I could never teach.'

===================

We accompanied Jehanne to the Church. Isabelle led the way and introduced the child to the Priest. Isabelle said her prayers and asked to be excused, a freedom which I was happy to grant.

We knelt near to the altar, and said our prayers. The Priest was surprised at the many prayers that our little one knew, and asked her age. 'Jehanne is four and a half years old,' I answered. 'I have been looking after her since birth. We are pleased that she is finally strong enough to be returned home to her family. Jehanne is devout; she is naturally full of good ways. She is already asking about the sacraments.'

The Priest replied that Jacques and Isabelle d'Arc had come to him, seeking to have an official baptism[53] performed in the very near future.

We left the Church with his blessing, knowing that we would often spend time there.

---

[53] Jehanne was baptised in Domrémy in 1412, which may be the reason why she was thought to have been born there and in that year.

Chapter XXV

Catharine at Poissy
And in Paris

- 1416 - 1417 -

*'Unto Thee, O Lord do I lift up my soul.
O my God, I trust in Thee...*[54]

My cherished friend Marie, Christine de Pisan's daughter, took up the religious life in 1397 at Poissy, the same year that Princess Marie, the five-year-old daughter of Isabeau de Bavière, was dedicated to God's service there. Christine was a frequent visitor to that convent.

It was in May 1416 that a messenger, dressed as a friar, appeared at the d'Arc home. He had been sent by the Prioress Princess Marie from Poissy, by special arrangement. Jacques d'Arc assembled all of us, and advised us. 'Our French army is under serious attack by the English, the battle at Agincourt last October, has been lost, costing the lives of 10,000 of our countrymen, including our most noble knights. Even our Charles d'Orléans has been taken prisoner by the English. He is now in England. We are advised to remain vigilant and very cautious of anyone seeking aid in our region. The convent at Poissy is now under English domination.'

---
[54] Psalm 25.

Jacques then handed me a letter from Christine, who was then staying at Poissy. Christine also mentioned the dire straits of our country. Paris continued to be in chaos, crippled with the influx of refugees coming from Normandy. Famine was spreading, taxes increased again and money devalued. Queen Isabeau was ignoring the plight of France, conspiring with the English, consolidating her ambitious desires and her personal power. She had no regard for the tragedy that was France. She organised gala occasions hosted at l'Hôtel St-Pôl for the enemies of France. Worse than this, it became public knowledge that she and certain of her ladies-in-waiting continued to disguise themselves as prostitutes and pay visit to the University at the Sorbonne, consorting with clerics and professors.

This information saddened me, but having previously observed Isabeau, it did not surprise me. But I read on.

Christine wrote that my mother was slowly dying. She was of course unable to predict the time of her death, but urged me to journey now to Poissy to see her there, one final time.

====================

I withdrew to our bedchamber. I was deeply saddened. I was grateful that Margaret and the d'Arc family were with me, and displayed true affection to my charge, the true little princess Jehanne, whose position seemed to me to be forever increasing in importance. Her protection was complete. I could indeed take leave from her, with peace in my heart.

=====================

I packed a few belongings and spoke with Jehanne. 'I must leave you, *ma Petite*, for a little while, as my own mother is dying and needs me. You will be cared for here, both by your mother and your father, and by Margaret. I look forward to seeing how you will have grown, inside and out, by the time I get back.'

I dressed myself in a simple grey linen tunic, and departed with the friar who had brought the messages to us. We took our leave, and easily joined a group of pilgrims who were also taking this much used trade route towards Paris.

The Arc family prayed for our safety.

======================

I arrived at Poissy in late June. Christine was the first to greet me. I saw tension in her whole being, even in this haven that was the convent.

'Ah, Catharine, I am so relieved that you have come. Marie will be so pleased to see her childhood companion. Princess Marie, who is now our Prioress, will welcome you. She is grateful for all of the good works that your mother has performed for this convent.

'And now we must speak of your mother. You will find her much changed. Her physical strength is gone. She is very frail. Her eyes are failing and her hearing is poor. I feel her need to transmit sacred knowledge, but I know that you are the only suitable recipient. I will take you to her now; she is in the infirmary in her own little room.'

We entered. There was a simple wooden cross above her bed. My mother was clutching a small statue of Our Lady holding the Holy Infant. Christine was correct; my mother was much diminished, nearly disappearing from our mortal view. She also held her old Cathar Rosary in her hands; she normally kept it hidden on her person, but today she needed to touch it. I kissed her on her forehead, noticing the scent of rosewater, my favourite scent from childhood. She had been bathed in it to the very last. Christine left us on our own.

She opened her eyes as I kissed her again. In a quiet voice, she said, 'Catharine, I have waited for you. I needed you to come to me to perform the Consolamentum to prepare me for my departure from this world. But first we must share some thoughts.

'I want you to know that my life has been a shaded light. I

could not openly live my Faith. But I have been accepted in this convent where I have been able to safely practice my beliefs, shielded by the official Church. I have been allowed to reside with nature, and to nurture plants that heal. I have been *Une Bonne Femme*[55]. You are also *Une Bonne Femme*, my Catharine. You know that you can confide most things in Christine, but be wary about your Faith, to keep it alive, forever. Her way is near to ours, but not exactly the same.

'She has shared many things with me also. I know about my granddaughter, and I am relieved that she is safe with the Orléans family. I am grateful to Christine for her friendship with Valentina Visconti that made this possible. I know about your current grave responsibilities; I know that the future of our France may well be in your hands.

'I have had visions. I remember that you escaped fire as a child. I know that for your royal child you will again face fire.' I was bewildered by these words, but dared not interrupt her flow of thoughts with any question.

I heard a tremor in her throat, and took her hands into mine. She handed me an old smallish volume from which she asked me to read. I recognised words therein; they were from the Gospel of Saint John. I touched her brow with the book. Then we said the prayers of Consolamentum. After this moment, my mother could receive no further sustenance as she had entered the Endura[56], but she did not crave anything. Her eyes held a light, which was focussed very far away. She was departing. I knelt and prayed with confidence for her soul, and also for all those I cherished, both living and departed. She was gone when I again raised my eyes; I closed hers. I put the book and her Rosary in a pocket under my ample skirts. I wept; sorrow overcame me. I had lost the roots of my life.

======================

Princess Marie organised a special Mass for her, which was

---

[55] term used for the Cathar faithful: Bon Homme, Bonne Femme
[56] fasting until death

attended by everyone at the convent. Both Christine and her daughter Marie de Castel led us in prayers. The choir of nuns sang her favourite psalms. According to her wishes, and by special dispensation, my mother was buried near her beloved garden at Poissy.

=====================

Marie de Castel sought me out afterwards. We strolled together in my mother's well-kept garden. 'Catharine,' she said, 'I have missed your energetic company here. My favourite childhood memories are of our time together. Do not misunderstand, I love my life here at Poissy. Perhaps this is a selfish petition, but I would like you to consider joining this convent. I think also of your safety. I know that the Prioress Princess Marie needs someone to fill your mother's position, and I cannot think of anyone better qualified than you.'

My friend Marie did not know that I had already had such a conversation with the royal Prioress. The Princess had asked me to assume my mother's vocation; I had already refused, agreeing only to stay for a period of time, to teach and guide my mother's previous assistant Agnes, to take on the work.

'Dear Marie, ' I answered, 'I fear that the path of my life has already been chosen for me. I will depart from Poissy as soon as Agnes is prepared. But I promise you, Marie, that I will visit you again.'

=====================

Christine spoke to me, 'You know your mother held a very special place in my heart. I am so pleased that I was able to be with her as her life was ebbing away. I can honestly say that she has been the only woman who has been able to understand my life and my struggle, a struggle which all loving widows, share.'

I answered her, expressing my gratitude, '*Chère Madame*

Christine, I am forever grateful to you and will never forget the day when you took us in and you agreed to guide me with your wisdom and your words. You have changed the course of my life.'

A smile broke out on her face. 'Catharine, you were always eager and have learnt your lessons well. I also know your heart; I know that you are anxious to return to Domrémy.'

Christine continued to speak her urgent words to me. 'I have recently had a message from the Palace,' she said. 'I am advised that there is again need of your midwifery services there. This time the mother-to-be is not Isabeau, but rather one of her ladies-in-waiting.'

====================

I could not refuse Christine, and embarked soon after on a journey to Paris, to the Château Vincennes. It was late March 1417.

====================

I arrived at Vincennes, and was escorted directly to the bedchamber of Queen Isabeau's lady. She was clearly quite some time away from her delivery. The lady in question was someone I had seen before. She was one of Isabeau's troupe of close companions who accompanied her on visits to the Sorbonne! She was already uncomfortable, I thought, because of disease, a result of her endless and irresponsible sexual behaviour. I quickly realised that I had been summoned under false pretences. The urgency of this confinement was not to deliver a child, but to abort it. She had already begun this abortion when I arrived: a heavy flow of blood was my first warning. The soft wooden stick she had used lay bloodied by her side.

I had no choice but to help, at great risk to my life and to my very soul. I was aided by unpractised servants, secretly commandeered. My confidence was shaken; these helpers were hysterical and incapable of responding to my directions.

The woman suddenly screamed and propelled the small being from her body. I collected the issue from between her out-stretched legs, and saw that it was dead. I quickly baptised it silently, and then went to aid her. Sadly her loss of blood was excessive, and she was losing her life. I spoke gently to her, and begged her to pray and ask forgiveness for her sins. I assured her that God is merciful, and that he would not reject her. She nodded and accepted my prayers. I was grateful that I had been able to secure a place for her in heaven, far preferable in my view, to life in the hell on earth that Isabeau administered.

I washed her and the baby to prepare them for burial. I lay the infant between her breasts so that they would be buried together. I admonished those traumatised helpers never to reveal what they had seen; they were correctly fearful, and finally able to respond to my commands. I told them to call for help to remove the bodies.

===================

As I left the room, I was suddenly confronted by Bois-Bourdon. He was more handsome than I remembered, and over-confident in his own importance. His bearing reflected his renowned bravery at Agincourt, which had gained him further favour at Court. 'Catharine,' he said, 'how delightful that you have arrived. I see that my entreaty to have you here has been well and convincingly conveyed.'

I was stunned by this encounter; but my response was not what he would have imagined. As I gazed upon him, I saw lines of impending torture in his face. He could not know what I saw; he laughed at his unbeknownst sorrowful future.

He tried to draw me into another room, and to take me in his arms; but I would not have him. I saw images in my mind that prevented me. I saw my mother, at her last; I saw Margaret, I saw my Christine Valentine, I saw Valentina Visconti; and finally I saw my Jehanne. I touched the book and the rosary in my pocket, knowing that I was already firmly on the long path to become a *Parfaite*. I could not be with him.

He did not understand; but then he was still resident in Isabeau's web.

I did take advantage of this moment with him, despite withdrawing from his amorous attentions. The event that had just past had alarmed me; I knew that I needed to return to Domrémy. I asked him to aid me in organising my return journey to Poissy, not wishing him to know my true destination. He promised to make the arrangements for me.

==================

It was not many days after when the King arrived unannounced at Vincennes. He saw Bois-Bourdon departing the Queen's bedchamber. Bois was very much in disarray, and neglected to show any respect to the King.

'Arrest that insolent scoundrel!' said the King. 'I know that it is Bois-Bourdon! He has now paid his last visit to my wife's bedchamber. Take him to Châtelet!'

During his questioning, Bois-Bourdon revealed more than anyone wanted to know. Arrogantly he produced the ring that Isabeau had given him at the very start of their affair; the Queen's token could not save him. It only served to confirm his treachery and hers. That very same evening Bois-Bourdon was condemned to die. He was sewn into a leather bag. The words inscribed thereon were: THE JUSTICE OF THE KING HAS BEEN CARRIED OUT. With this act, the Queen's ambitious, manipulative partner was dropped into the Seine.

A few days later, under the orders of her son, Charles[57], Isabeau was forcibly sent to Blois and then to Tours for a period of exile, under the close supervision of three severe guardians, who treated her with no respect and no consideration.

Charles the Dauphin was at this time, without resources. He took advantage of his mother's rich wardrobe, fabulous jewels, and valuable furniture which were left behind when she was

---

[57] Charles became the Dauphin in April 1417 after the death of Jean.

escorted from Vincennes. He sold her belongings to replenish the coffers of the Armagnacs, but sadly it was not enough. Some of his Armagnac followers deserted and joined the Burgundians. At the same time, Henry V landed in Normandy, sure of the support of Jean sans Peur. He marched with this ally to Paris, stopping at Senlis, with a demand that Charles VI cede him the Crown of France, with the proviso that Charles VI might be King until the end of his life. Henry V would then be Regent. Henry demanded the hand of Charles VI's daughter, Catherine, for his queen, to serve as the Seal of their Agreement. At that moment Charles VI was sane, and took these matters under due consideration.

Isabeau tired of her exile, managed to enlist the aid of a servant to conduct her out of Tours to attend Mass at Marmoutier, where she was rescued by Hector de Sauveuse, an aide of Jean sans Peur. She was reunited with him soon afterwards.

In her anger, she confided in Jean sans Peur. She shared with him her truth that Charles le Dauphin was not the son of the King, but the son of her brother-in-law Louis, and hence had no right to the throne of France.

The following day, the Queen forced the town of Tours to surrender to Jean sans Peur, Duc de Bourgogne. He was accepted with jubilation as the crowds thought that peace would be theirs, and the reunited couple continued their procession to Chartres. On the strength of his support, Isabeau declared herself Regent and established her Court at Troyes.

======================

My head was bursting with the events of this moment. I was grateful that I had had the presence of mind to get Bois-Bourdon to organise my departure, in advance of his own permanent one.

I left Vincennes with all discretion and haste, happy again to reach the solace of Poissy.

I went directly to Christine and told her that I had been the victim of a deception. I also told her all that I could recall of the royal double dealings. Christine was grateful to remain in the safety of the convent where she could entirely avoid the Court.

As always, Christine calmed me and helped me. I was soon on my way back to Domrémy.

Chapter XXVI

Jehanne at Domrémy

Saints Catharine, Margaret and Michael

1417 - 1421

'Save me, O God, by thy name, and judge me by thy strength.
Hear my prayer, O God; give ear to the words of my mouth.'[58]

The pastoral countryside of Domrémy was most welcoming after the intrigues and chaos of Paris. My time away from Jehanne had been such a long and sad one, seeing her again was a joy and a blessing. She had grown beautifully under Margaret's care, and was thriving as a fit country person. Her physical strength was increasing, she was able to cope as well as her brothers, running through the fields and tending the animals. She was also beginning to learn the rudimentary skills of spinning and weaving, thanks to the able tutelage of Isabelle d'Arc.

She was healthy and devout, attending Mass every morning, readily confessing her sins, and communing every year, as was

---

[58] Psalm 54

the custom. She did not know why she typically prayed the 'Our Father' nine times, but no one assigned any importance to it.

I spoke to Margaret secretly. We decided that our ten year old Jehanne was at the age where we could begin to suggest some truths to her. We decided that we would use the narcotic herbs that grew all around us. My skills with plants and herbs would be very useful once again.

We began our appointed mission in the spring of 1418.

We would work in secret, inducing a hypnotic dream-like state in Jehanne. We needed for her to understand who she was, and the potential importance of her role in France. Mandrake was the ingredient we chose; from it we made a sweet syrup that would induce a dream-like sleep. I was grateful for my mother's skilful instruction in its preparation.

We began very slowly, telling her first that she was of royal birth, and that her true father was Louis d'Orléans, and that her birth mother was Queen Isabeau. It was only after the death of Valentina that we had to take her to Domrémy for protection to be provided by Jacques d'Arc, who was well compensated for taking on the role of her father in this life. She must always remember who she is; but when she awakened, she would be unable remember any of the specific suggestions made to her.

I was also grateful for the instruction that I had received, even as a child, from Christine. I was pleased to be able to base Jehanne's education in respect of comportment, on Christine's works, *Le Livre des Trois Vertus*, and *La Cité des Dames*[59] which Christine had given me some time ago. Educating Jehanne about the events of our times, fell to me, and to my observations and to the communications that we received here in Domrémy. Some messages were delivered to us directly from Christine.

Once she had got into bed, I would say, 'Jehanne, drink this

---

[59] Christine de Pisan's books were inspired by her dreams, and we thought it fitting that we teach Jehanne in her dreams, using Christine's works.

strengthening potion. It will help you to sleep and to dream God's truths.' And then we would hand her a goblet of warm milk, into which we had blended the syrup of the sacred, powerful Mandrake root. She always responded with trust and compliance, and she always proposed that we should pray together just after. We would kneel together, Jehanne, Margaret, and I, and say the 'Our Father.' Then she would pray for all her family and for our beautiful France. And then a sleep-like state would overtake her.

Margaret would whisper to me. 'I am certain that I know the content of your prayers, Catharine.' 'Yes, Margaret, I believe that we must now shape and guide this life, which has been entrusted to us. I believe that she is ready to accept our words.'

I would touch her hand. 'Jehanne, this is your Catharine. I speak to you now. We have mentioned to you before that our King and indeed our France could be usurped. You are going to be the saviour of our Fair Land. At the battle of Agincourt, Henry V, King of England, has already taken a large portion of our country. Our Queen Isabeau has convinced her mad husband, to offer their daughter Princess Catharine, as his bride. Without intervention, he will become the heir to the French throne.

'Isabeau has only one surviving son, Charles, who could be a contender for the throne. He is your true brother, as you both have the same father and the same mother. Your father Louis d'Orléans had the foresight to place you directly into the care of his wife, Valentina.

'You, Jehanne, have been protected all your life, since an early age looked after by the parents that Valentina chose for you. You must know in your heart that you are truly a princess.

'When you awaken, you will be aware of a need to seek out Charles. You will succeed in reaching him, even though you must cross enemy lines. Your strength will be limitless. You will be indistinguishable from the men who will serve under you. It will take some time for you to be prepared for your important role, but you will acquire the skills and the wit to succeed. You, my child, will save France.'

Margaret gazed at me, and was astonished to see the change of expression on my face. She had been unaware of my knowledge about the times and Jehanne's destiny.

Then Margaret would speak with her. She took her hands in her own. '*Ma petite Jehanne*, every time you hear the bells chime the Angelus, at 6:00 in the morning, at midday, and at 6:00 in the evening, your heart will be filled with great strength and you will feel palpitations. You will pray to our Lady and to Jesus. Then you will hear my voice, guiding your thoughts to your life's tasks. You are the only one who will hear our voices, mine and Catharine's. You must not reveal these truths to anyone. You know that we are messengers of God, and you can rely on the shield of our love.'

Each night after imparting these dreams to Jehanne, we were exhausted. We kissed her gently, and went off to our beds.

Each morning thereafter, Jehanne would rush from her bed at the morning chime of the Angelus. She would kneel and pray devoutly, and give the appearance of someone hurrying, with great urgency.

=================

One morning in 1420, our efforts came to fruition. Jehanne awakened just before the Angelus, and awaited the chimes.

'I am called to pray, Catharine. This day I shall fast and go to Church to be confessed. I know that I must vow to God to remain a maid, for as long as it will please Him.'

'Why do you fast, Jehanne?' I asked.

'Today, Catharine, I know more about my calling. I feel it. I know that I will soon know how I shall succeed.'

I accompanied her to Mass; she was so very focussed in her devotions.

We returned home; Margaret stretched out her hand,

offering her a mug of milk. Jehanne refused it.

I had to tell Margaret that Jehanne had decided to fast today, and that she had made a vow, offering herself to God, for His purposes.

==================

We took up the lessons; we gently encouraged Jehanne to speak her mind.

Margaret said, 'Dear Jehanne, we have read many lessons to you over these years. Today, as it is a day you have chosen, we would like to hear you read what you have copied from the Holy Books in our Church. We know that you have been busy with it, and we hope that you are ready to share it with us now.'

'Of course, dear Margaret and Catharine. I shall try. I have chosen the Gospel of Saint John.[60] I have these words:

"And we have known and believed the love that God hath to us. God is love; and he that dwelleth in love dwelleth in God, and God in him. Herein is our love made perfect, that we may have boldness in the day of judgement; because as He is, so are we in this world. There is no fear in love; but perfect love casteth out fear: because fear hath torment. He that feareth is not made perfect in love. We love Him because He first loved us. If a man say, I love God and hateth his brother, he is a liar; for he that loveth not his brother whom he hath seen, how can he love God whom he hath not seen? And this commandment have we from Him, That he who loveth God love his brother also."

We listened and were gladdened by the passage she had chosen. Her wisdom was well beyond her twelfth year.

Margaret reminded her to exercise caution in her pursuit of learning. We taught her by example, and she was an exemplary pupil.

Jehanne responded, 'Of course I know in my heart that I must serve France and expel the English from our lands. I am

---

[60] The Gospel of Saint John was the gospel favoured by the Cathars.

certain that I must fight our enemy, but I do not yet know how I shall achieve this. I have faith; I believe that God guides my every step. We must have our freedom from the English.'

She was almost too impetuous. 'Dear Jehanne,' I answered, 'what you dream may be difficult. But as God is in you and always with you, I am also certain that you will succeed. You are truly the Maid of France and a Child of God.'

==================

On an afternoon in summer 1421, a moment when there was a lull in the Hundred Year conflict, Jehanne was seated under a special tree with Margaret and me, reading her lessons out-of-doors. Suddenly there appeared in front of us, a known yet unknown figure of a young man, silhouetted against the sun. Jehanne recognised him straight away as she had seen him at various Orléans functions before. She leapt up to extend her exuberant greeting to Jehan, Comte de Dunois, the well-known Bastard of Orléans. With great joy Margaret and I also rose, and embraced him in greeting.

He was very special for us, as Valentina Visconti had accepted him as one of her own. He was now the acting head of the Orléans household.[61]

We had heard rumours of his impending arrival, but had no certainty about the time frame, as the enemy lines were very close to Domrémy. We were not only pleased to see him, but relieved.

Jehanne was full of questions for Jehan. 'What a lovely surprise to see you here. Have you done well in battle for our fair France?'

Jehan looked at all of us, before responding. 'The battles have been difficult. I was imprisoned by the Burgundians in the Château de Saint Germaine, finally freed by Jean sans Peur two years ago.'

Jehanne, unable to contain her enthusiasm, declared, 'I am

---

[61] Charles d'Orléans was imprisoned in England, since his capture at Agincourt in 1415.

so pleased to see you again, but I must say that I do not like it that your name is so similar to my own. And I do not like it that you are known simply as the Bastard of Orléans. I have decided,' she said in a voice with great determination and purpose, 'that I shall call you Michael. It is a good, strong name, after the powerful Archangel.[62] And Catharine has just told me that l'Isle Saint Michel still belongs to our Fair France.'

Jehan laughed and answered, 'All right, Jehanne, for you my name is henceforth Michael. What can I do for you, my little sister?' he said smiling and bowing deeply.

'Tell me about your righteous battles, dear Michael,' she answered. 'I need to know what life is like on the battlefield? How do you manage? How do you fight? How do you get your men to follow you? And, most importantly, how do you win? What is the source of your inspiration? Is it Our Lord? These questions have been wearing on me for quite some time.'

'Why should such things occupy your thoughts, dear sweet Jehanne? Surely you spend your time in prayer and song. You should soon be thinking of marriage. I will be happy to help to arrange a good match for you.'

'Michael,' said Jehanne, 'you must understand: I know that I am called by our Lord, the King of Heaven, to serve our earthly king in battle, and to deliver France to his care. I shall see to it that Charles is anointed with the sacred oils in Rheims. I am not just a simple maid.'

Michael was shocked, but the tone of Jehanne's voice and the extraordinary light in her eyes convinced him that she was divinely inspired and earnestly serious. He responded to her determined needs. 'In that case, I shall teach you the art of knighthood. You will learn in a few hours what has taken a lifetime to instil in others because your mind has the fervour and the faith and the vision to guide you to save the Crown of France.'

---

[62] Michael the Archangel leads the hosts of Heaven to battle against Satan. He is depicted with a flaming sword and sometimes with a pair of scales. His Feast Day is celebrated on the 29th September.

Margaret and I, in deep understanding with Jehan, handed him some herbs, knowing that they would be needed to achieve what he had promised.

'Michael, you know me. I fanatically adhere to the commands of God. I hear them with my whole being. I will take your instructions and be empowered, in praise of the King of Heaven and of our Noble Charles.'

Jehan was still somewhat wary about the journey he was aiding Jehanne to set upon, but assured her and himself, 'Under the guidance and protection of Catharine, Margaret, and me, you will be strengthened in thought, word, purpose, and deed.'

Jehanne was confident, 'I thank you in advance. I follow you, Michael.... I have known my mission, but I have not known before this day how to equip myself to accomplish it.'

BOOK IX

The Historic Epiphany:

Observations of an Anonymous Chronicler

Chapter XXVII

Isabeau and the Kingdom of France

1418 - 1422

'Why boastest thou thyself in mischief, O mighty man?
The goodness of God endureth continually.
The tongue deviseth mischiefs; like a sharp razor,
working deceitfully.
Thou lovest evil more than good; and lying rather than to
speak righteousness…'[63]

It is known from the *Journal du Menagier de Paris*[64], that the situation in Paris reached a nadir, commencing in 1418. The Burgundians had taken Paris. They had arrived in stealth to massacre the Armagnacs and to undermine the Dauphin Charles.

Queen Isabeau had appointed herself Regent from the time she had established her Court at Troyes. She was supported in her endeavours by Jean sans Peur.

Charles VI resided in the Palais du Louvre; it mattered little to him that his country was in turmoil, as he was a prisoner of his own mind. He barely noticed the events that surrounded him, apart from the fact that Isabeau had grown grossly fat and ugly.

---
[63] Psalm 52
[64] Writings about the reign of Charles VI and Charles VII

The Dauphin Charles had been dragged in his sleep from l'Hôtel Neuf. He was moved a safe distance away to Melun.

====================

By September 1419, Isabeau's anger had overtaken her. She had been trying for some time to find a way to have Charles, her only remaining son, assassinated. She engaged her ally Jean sans Peur to carry it out.

Isabeau devised a plan. 'My heart will not rest, ' she said to Jean sans Peur, 'until you have succeeded in assassinating my son, the so-called Dauphin[65]. I have already planned this murder meticulously. I have sent a message to Charles in your name that he should meet you to discuss an interview with his father. In this meeting, I rely on you. Do not threaten him with gestures, only with words, so that his guards will not be alarmed. Raise your voice just at the end, so that your guards are instantly summoned to defend you, by attacking him. He shall then be killed by 'accident'.'

Jean sans Peur was happy to have the opportunity to comply. The rendez-vous was set to occur at the Bridge of Montereau near Paris, on the 10th September 1420, where the Dauphin had erected a tent at one end.

Jean sans Peur did as Isabeau instructed. He declared, 'Charles, you are commanded to pay respect to your father.'

Charles had little interest in the words of anyone so closely aligned to his mother. 'I need not pay heed to your requests or commands. You are not my lord or master. I do not need your advice.'

Jean sans Peur put his hand on Charles' collar and the other on his sword. Charles screamed, and when his servant saw that his master appeared to be threatened, he ran to his aid, pushing the Duc out of the tent, and then shattering his skull with an axe. Charles did not witness the actual slaughter of his cousin, who died instantly.

---

[65] 'So-called Dauphin' was an appellation coined in all probability by Pierre Cauchon., Bishop of Beauvais and private secretary to Queen Isabeau.

When he did exit the tent, Charles saw the body, and wept, knowing that not only was his cousin lost, but that he would bear the blame for his death.[66]

====================

Isabeau was deeply grieved that her plan had gone awry.

She had previously disliked and disowned her son, but now she detested him; she was angry that he was still alive. He had deprived her of her final lover. She reflected on her condition. She was now old, over 50 years. Her body had thickened, her limbs were enlarged. Her face was no longer pleasant to gaze upon. She was certain that she could no longer find a lover; her increasing desires would go unsatisfied. She mourned her Jean.

Her sole mission became a crusade to turn the whole of France against the Dauphin, her bastard son, before the death of her husband, Charles VI.

She was determined give the Crown of France to England.[67]

====================

On the 22nd August 1422, the body of King Henry V was carried out of the Palace at Vincennes. He had mysteriously fallen ill, and died of apparent food poisoning. Catherine, his wife, daughter of Queen Isabeau and Charles VI, grieved alone, in London.

Soon after, on the 22nd October 1422, without ever regaining his sanity, Charles VI died in his bedchamber at

---

[66] Philippe de Bourgogne, son of Jean sans Peur, certain of support from Henry V, declared the Dauphin Charles to be disinherited from his right of succession. Philippe married Michelle, daughter of Isabeau. Michelle expressed her great affection for her brother Charles, and was poisoned by direction of Isabeau on the 8th July 1422. Henry V offered Philippe the position of Regent upon the death of Charles VI; Philippe refused.

[67] The Crown of France was ceded to Henry V, King of England on the 20th May 1420 by the Treaty of Troyes. Charles VI was to remain King in name only until his death; Isabeau would remain Regent also until the death of Charles VI.

l'Hôtel St-Pôl.

God bless the soul of Henry V. God bless the soul of Charles VI, our gentle King. God bless the new infant king[68], Henry VI, son of Henry V and Catherine of France, now King of France and England.

There were other prayers: to bless the Dauphin Charles, who resided at this time in Poitiers, in hiding. His faithful followers nominated him Charles VII.[69]

---

[68] He was nine months old.
[69] Charles was also affectionately called le Petit Roi de Bourges by his retinue.

Chapter XXVIII

Jehanne

1429

'Blessed be the Lord my strength,
Which teacheth my heart to war, and my fingers to fight:
My goodness, and my fortress; my high tower, and
my deliverer;
My shield, and He in whom I trust....'[70]

Jehanne was well trained by this time, and filled with the strength of her conviction. She made a practical plan to follow. She knew that she would first have to convince Robert de Baudricourt, the governor of Vaucouleurs, of her divinely inspired mission, and that she was God's true instrument.

She had known Baudricourt since childhood, but he had consistently ignored her. She petitioned him twice; but it was not until February of 1429 that he actually paid heed to her words. 'The kingdom of France does not belong to the Dauphin, but to the Lord God of Heaven. Our Lord wills that the Dauphin shall be made King and have custody of the kingdom. And I shall lead him to his anointing.'

Robert de Baudricourt was finally convinced. He

---
[70] Psalm 144

responded, 'Your conviction is clear; although I have refused you before, and chastised you to return to your father, I now give you a sword, as you requested, and also, the male costume you require. You will be escorted to Chinon, to the court of the Dauphin.'

By this time, he had heard the rumour that the Kingdom of France was already betrayed and lost by a woman, that woman being the treacherous Isabeau de Bavière. The prophesy continued, that the Kingdom of France could be saved by a virgin, mounted on horse-back. He was concerned that this very virgin could be Jehanne, standing before him at this moment. He dared not be the one to oppose her.

===================

After an arduous journey through territories held by the English, Jehanne arrived at the Court of the Dauphin, at Chinon in Touraine, on the 6th March 1429. She was accompanied by only two men, Jean de Metz and Bertrand de Poulengy[71], sent by Robert de Baudricourt.

She went directly to the Court, expecting to notice the Dauphin, perhaps by distinctive dress, or by the deference paid him by others in the room. She began to approach the group in this Court, but stopped short, and then walked directly to the Dauphin.

'Gentle Dauphin[72], ' she said, ' I am known as Jehanne *La Pucelle*. My beloved and noble Dauphin, I do not fear the men of arms; I find the pathway clear and free for me. I have come a far distance to see you, and I have great things to reveal to you. I know you easily: you are clearly distinguished to me from all men.'

The Dauphin was taken aback, at being so directly recognised and addressed. 'What if I am not the Dauphin?

---

[71] In the service of the Queen of Sicily, Yolande d'Aragon, mother-in-law to Charles le Dauphin.
[72] Source of quotes, paraphrased responses: JOAN OF ARC – In Her Own Words, compiled and translated by William Trask Afterward by Sir Edward S. Creasy, BOOKS & CO., Turtle Point Press, New York 1996

Perhaps he is that lord standing over there......'

Jehanne, answered him, not without impatience, 'In God's name, it is you, and none other. I am sent to you by God to save you and your kingdom. The King of Heaven commands that through me you shall be anointed and crowned at Rheims. I say to you, on behalf of the Lord, that you are the true heir of France.'

====================

Charles was shocked both by her confident words and her approach. He had never been addressed in this way. He also noticed that Jehanne and he shared physical likeness.[73] He had long suffered under the possibility that he might not be the legitimate heir to the throne; in fact his mother Queen Isabeau had told him this. It was indeed unlikely that Charles VI had been able to father him. Jehanne could be the living proof that he had a real sibling, reinforcing the worry that he had not been fathered by the king. He took Jehanne aside, and they spoke intensively.

'My Liege, I perceive that you are as surprised as I am by how similar we look. You are my brother; I have often wondered about the circumstances of my birth. My voices have maintained that I am of royal blood, although I have not understood before how that could be.'

Charles answered, 'My mother is our Queen Isabeau. My mother has told me that I am a bastard. At the time of my conception, my father was mad. My true father was his brother, Louis d'Orléans. My mother told me this: that is why at the Treaty of Troyes I was called a bastard and the Crown of France was ceded to our half-sister Catherine who married Henry V of England. Now that Henry V is dead, their child, Henry VI of England, Henry II of France was named King in 1422, at the age of 9 months. I escaped to Bourges.

---

[73] There were three characteristics that made their likeness clear. They were: a small scarlet marking behind the right ear; each speaks in a measured way, very calmly; and a longish neck, head held high, which was a characteristic of the princes of the Valois-Orléans family

'You, Jehanne, must be the child of my mother, that she was given to believe was born dead.'

Jehanne answered him, 'I shall win the crown of France for you, and I shall get the holy oils to anoint you in Rheims as the true King of France. You are the only true heir to this title. God wills it. We will shatter the rule of England over our land.'

====================

On the 22nd March 1429, Jehanne wrote to the King of England, and to all of his representatives.

> "Jesus – Maria
> King of England, and you, Duke of Bedford,
> Who call yourself Regent of the Kingdom of France,
> You, William de la Poule, Earl of Suffolk;
> Sir John Talbot, and,
> You, Sir Thomas of Scales,
> Who call yourself Lieutenant of the aforesaid Duke of Bedford,
> Render your account to the King of Heaven.
> Surrender to the Maid, who is sent here by God the King of Heaven,
> The keys of all the good towns you have captured and destroyed in France...
> And you should know for sure that the King of Heaven will send more strength
> To the Maid than you are able to put against her and her good soldiers
> in any attack. And when the blows begin, it will be clear who is in the right
> Before the God of Heaven..."[74]

====================

---

[74] source of this quote and the others of Jehanne that follow: **JOAN OF ARC - IN HER OWN WORDS**, compiled and translated by Willard Trask, B•O•O•K•S & Co., TURTLE POINT PRESS, New York, 1996, Library of Congress Number 95-080863, ISBN 1-885983-08-5

On the 29th April 1429, just before the Liberation d'Orléans, Jehanne was organising her troops for the attack.

It was Jehan, Comte de Dunois, the Bastard of Orléans, who approached her. 'Jehanne La Pucelle, I join your quest.'

She answered him, pretending not to know that she had ever met him before. 'Are you the Bastard of Orléans? Was it you that counselled that we should come here on this side of the river, and not go to where John Talbot and the English are?'

'Yes, I, and others wiser than I, believe that it is safer and surer,' he answered.

Her leadership challenged on this point, Jehanne answered: 'In God's name! Our Lord God's counsel is surer and wiser than yours. You thought to deceive me; it is yourself you deceive. For I bring you better succour than ever came to captain or town, which is succour from the King of Heaven. Nor is it granted for love of me; but God, at the prayer of Saint Louis and Saint Charlemagne, has taken pity on the town of Orléans, nor will He suffer the enemy to hold both the Duc d'Orléans' person and his town.'

The matter settled, Jehanne turned to face the people. She raised her arms and spoke: 'My Lord has sent me to succour this good town of Orléans. Hope in God. If you have good hope and faith in Him, you shall be delivered from your enemies.'

Orléans was completely liberated under her leadership on the 8th May 1429. She was truly the Maid of Orléans, both by her heredity and by her deeds.

=====================

Sometime after these events, Yolanda[75], mother-in-law to Charles, initiated a conversation with him: 'Charles,' she said, 'I think you now know that Jehanne is Blessed by God. She will fulfil the ancient prophecy. You gave her only the remnants of an army and she has taken Orléans for you. You must accord her praise and position, and the support of your

---

[75] Yolanda d'Aragon was married to Louis II, Duc d'Anjou and King of Naples and Sicily; in her own right she was the Duchess of Bar and the Queen of Aragon.

best soldiers. She is without malice, without suspicion. She is innocence itself, her trust in the King of Heaven, and in you, is without condition and without parallel.'

Charles agreed in principle, but maintained that he also had his favourite courtiers upon whom he relied for advice.

Yolanda was adamant. 'Your favourite courtiers only flatter and deceive you. They do nothing to support your reign. Jehanne has promised to anoint you with the sacred oils at Rheims and to crown you as the one true king of France. How can you doubt her?'

====================

Jehanne knew that this victory was only one step in her mission. She had made her promise to the Dauphin and to her Lord, the King of Heaven. She was convinced that he must be anointed with the holy oils and crowned at Rheims, for that in so doing, he would be assured of legitimacy, and victories in his name would occur.

Jehanne, Jehan the Comte Dunois, and Gilles de Rais[76] met at Château Neuf sur Loire with Charles the Dauphin on the 24th June. There, after several days' discussion, they agreed to the march to Rheims which was Jehanne's determined path. There was one important obstacle at Troyes: the supporters of Philippe le Bon de Bourgogne and his ally John, the Duke of Bedford. A charismatic Franciscan preacher, brother Richard intervened and smoothed their way. They arrived jubilantly at Rheims on Saturday the 16th July. They had little time to organise the event, as, in keeping with sacred tradition, the coronation would have to occur on a Sunday, in fact, the very next day.

The witnesses were to be the various bishops representing France; because of the short notice many had to be replaced. The most notable of the missing was Pierre Cauchon, the Bishop of Beauvais: he should have been in attendance as he

---

[76] Wealthy companion of Jehanne, supported the coronation of Charles VII, made Marshall of France and later condemned by Charles VII, in folklore eventually became associated with Blue Beard, wife murderer.

was responsible to the Archbishop of Rheims. The solid gold crown did not arrive in time; a substitute from the vaults of the Church had to be used. The ampoule of holy oil was delivered by an abbot from St Remi on the 17th, just in time on the actual day.

Charles VII was knighted, then anointed with the holy oils, and crowned.

'Gentle King, now is done the will of God who wanted me to lift the siege of Orléans and to bring you to this City of Rheims to receive your holy sacring showing that you are truly king, and he to whom the kingdom of the Franks should belong.' After she spoke these words, she broke down, knelt, embraced her brother round the legs, and was overcome with emotion.

====================

After these victorious events, Jehanne's divine inspiration[77] became legendary. She received a letter from the Duc d'Armagnac, requesting that she, with her clear guidance from God, advise him as to which of the then three Popes[78] was the correct one.

On the 29th August 1429, Jehanne replied by letter:

"I cannot make known to you the truth at present until I shall be in Paris, or elsewhere at peace. For I am at present too much prevented by the business of war. But when you learn that I am in Paris, send me a message and I shall make you to know in truth which one you should believe in, and you will have knowledge of it through the advice of my rightful sovereign Lord, the King of all the world."

---

[77] Divine inspiration was eventually turned against her, and she was labelled as a sorceress or employing witchcraft to achieve her noble ends.
[78] Clement VIII, Avignon; Martin V, Rome; Benedict XIV, Hidden

BOOK X

Catharine and Jehanne:

Closing the Circle

Chapter XXIX

Fate of Jehanne and Catharine

-- 1430 – 1431 --

'O God, make haste to my rescue,
Lord, come to my aid!
Let there be shame and confusion
On those who seek my life.'[79]

The inhabitants of Compiègne were calling for Jehanne to save them from the English and Burgundians who were approaching their city. She arrived there on the 22nd May, and on the afternoon of the 23rd May she decided to go out to assess the oncoming armies. Jehanne made it her mission to go onto the bridge over the moat, clearly at the most hazardous position. At about five o'clock in the afternoon, the Burgundians attacked. The governor of Compiègne closed the portcullis behind her, and she was easily de-horsed and captured by the attacking Burgundians. Perhaps this was the governor's act of treachery, but by sacrificing Jehanne, he safeguarded the population within the city's walls.

Jehanne was first taken to Château Beaulieu, then she was transferred to Château Beaurevoir, where she spent time in the

---

[79] Psalm 70

company of two pleasant ladies of Luxembourg, the wife and the aunt of Jean de Luxembourg in whose care she remained. He was an ally of the Burgundians. He was responsible for detaining her for four months in all. He sought to be compensated for his role as her gaoler. Before offering her to the English, he did the moral thing: he offered her to Charles VII. The support she had given him, and the support he owed her, was widely understood.

A messenger was sent to Charles VII. 'Noble King,' he said, 'I bring you a message from my Sire, the Count of Luxembourg. He has asked me to speak it so that none may steal any paper from me. He declares that he holds your Jehanne as prisoner. For a reasonable payment he will release her to you. He currently holds a bid also from the English, but gives you first right to her.'

Charles agreed to consider this proposition, and to send a messenger with his answer. But he never did.

===================

I, Catharine, tried very hard to keep up with Jehanne, at least close enough to know her news. At nearly the age of fifty, I had taken a moment of respite at Chinon before I learnt of her capture. I was wondering how I could reach her and help her, when my prayers were answered by the arrival of this messenger from Jean de Luxembourg. I decided to travel back to her side in his company.

I had to plan my approach to the Count, and to choose my words with great care.

The messenger was pleased to have my silent companionship for his return journey; I was lost in my thoughts.

We arrived at the Château Crotoy, castle of Jean de Luxembourg. He and his wife and aunt were seated in the grand hall.

I was announced on arrival. Jean was surprised to have a visitor, but allowed me to enter. I barely introduced myself, going directly to state the purpose of my presence.

'*Je suis Catharine la Lapine, sage femme et nourrice.* I have come to plead with you. You must keep Jehanne as your prisoner, we must be confident that she is safe from the enemies of France, from the enemies within the Church, and the other enemies at l'Université de Paris, specifically those associated with Charles who is under the domination of his favourites. They play on his insecurities and weaknesses. I know all this through Yolanda d'Aragon.'

Jean answered me, looking somewhat surprised to the words he was hearing, coming from one attired as a peasant. 'As you know, I have offered Jehanne to Charles, but my messenger has returned without his reply. The English and the Church will pay any price, to have her tried and condemned as a heretic and an impostor. She, who is adored by the good people of France, is at high risk.'

'If you sell her, it is you who will be condemned, forever.' I explained why, and then we agreed that I should present the information to Pierre Cauchon who was to arrive the next day. I was given sustenance and a bed, and awaited the next requirement to tell my tale. Jean de Luxembourg and I agreed that Jehanne must not know of my presence here.

====================

Pierre Cauchon arrived and was greeted by Jean de Luxembourg. He began his mission, saying, 'I am under instructions of the most specific nature, given by the highest authorities. I have come to take Jehanne from you; I have brought the offered payment[80] from the Church and from England. I have been commanded to lead the trial to declare her a witch and a sorceress and a heretic in the eyes of the Church. Queen Isabeau is angry. She would have her burnt at the stake, as an enemy of France, an enemy of England, and an enemy of the Church.'

---

[80] The equivalent of £10,000 in gold.

Jean answered him, 'It is strange to think she who created the miracles for Charles, the liberation of Orléans and his coronation at Rheims, should be so punished. Perhaps King Charles is afraid that he could lose his crown to her.'

Cauchon was confused by this statement, 'How could that be? Charles has her to thank for his coronation and the confirmation of his position. She claims that she was guided by the Almighty. As the instrument of God she could have no other ambition.'

Jean had to answer, 'There is circumstance of which few are aware. Suffice it to say that Jehanne is of Royal Blood. I will now introduce you to a personage who will explain this secret to you. I charge you to listen, and at all costs, protect Jehanne from the official injustices, which will be required.

Cauchon was clearly taken aback. Jean then opened the door, and allowed me to enter. So as not to be compromised, Jean departed. I spoke courageously with my usual authority.

'Your Grace, I come to you with a knowledge that I must impart, much against my will. I will say this only once. Many years ago, in 1407, Isabeau, our Dowager Queen, was delivered of child, which was said to have been born dead, called Philippe. The truth is, that the child was a healthy female. I delivered her myself, and baptised her, Jehanne, fille de la Reine. She was the child of Isabeau and Louis d'Orléans, the King's brother. Louis was assassinated soon after. Valentina, his beloved wife, commanded me to escape from Paris with the child, as my own. I was chosen to nurture this child and to remain forever her companion.'

Whilst I was speaking these words, I was without pain and fear. My heart was racing as I was realising what I was proposing. Thoughts of my own married daughter Christine Valentine, visions of my three dear grandchildren interrupted my flow. But I was destined to save the Saviour of France. Panic hastened my words, I felt that God was within me.

I knew that I had no choice; I had loved Jehanne always. I continued, 'I will give myself to God after the official judgement condemns her. In return, you must swear, on all that is Holy, God our Father, Jesus Christ His Son, the Holy Spirit, and our Virgin Mother Mary, that you will keep her safe.'

Cauchon answered me, his demeanour alternating between astonishment and acceptance and comprehension, 'You do not surprise me, I have felt that Jehanne was always regal in composure and comportment. I have delayed completing the transaction to purchase her for the English and the Church. I was hoping to know the details that I have long suspected.

'I understand now... with your death you will take the guilt of France and England and the Church.... I wonder whether it will ever be acknowledged. The power of God which Jehanne reveres, has long been neglected in the Church and in the Monarchy: that I know only too well.'

He seemed to respond with genuine concern, although I knew that he was well practiced in the royal circles of treachery. I was still concerned that he might not be fully trustworthy. I admonished him, 'I trust you to keep your word and to act for God, the King of Heaven. I shall confirm our encounter and your success in a way that it will be known. I have given a pouch containing a personal token to Jean de Luxembourg which he will deliver to Christine de Pisan who will see to it that it reaches the hand of my daughter.' The token I was sending to Christine Valentine was my mother's Rosary. 'Christine will write a poem to honour Jehanne after my death, so that the world will believe her valiant deeds, forever after, without knowing that her life continues.'

===================

Jehanne was moved to the prison in Rouen; Jean de Luxembourg arranged for me to be with her there. She had an official cell, where she was held during the day. She was transferred each evening to better quarters when the English guards departed from their duty. I stayed with her, we prayed together, as always.

I cautioned her, 'My dear Jehanne, I advise you to say

nothing. Follow Jean de Luxembourg. He has contracted an understanding with your judges. Go with him, wherever he takes you.

'You cannot rely on Charles your brother, he is fearful about his own position and confused. Your birth mother, Queen Isabeau, does not even know that you are her child, the truth was hidden from her. Even as a warrior for France, she condemned you as an enemy of France, a traitor, and a witch.

'The arrangement is that after these trials that you must endure, a burning is expected, in fact it is Queen Isabeau who has suggested this outcome to the English and to the Church. She awaits the coronation of her grandson, young Henry, to whom she has given her pledge.'

As always, Jehanne took my words to heart, weeping daily. She still could not restrain her clever and spirited responses at her trial, knowing that the content of her words would not affect the outcome of what was pre-determined.

====================

On the 30th May 1431, Pierre Cauchon came to visit her in her cell at the Prison Beaurevoir, and she taunted him with her usual bravado: 'Am I to be taken now, to my death? Cauchon, I said before to you that I would surely die at your hand.'

Cauchon was somewhat nervous that he was then in the position to surreptitiously free her, and whispered to her, 'Quiet, Jehanne, be patient.'

I kissed her, now for the last time, with all the love I had always felt for this child. I had only a few more words to say to her, 'My dearest Jehanne, it is all arranged. In a few moments you will be spirited away. You are goodness and light; you do not belong here. Without you, my life is finished. I give myself the honour of taking your place at the stake. Live long and well, my child.' I kept the small book that my mother had given me at her death in my hands; I thought it should burn with me, the Spirit of the Word of Saint John to rise with my own. I quickly pressed my rosary into Jehanne's hands; she held it tightly, as if holding it enabled her to hold onto me. I managed to quickly say the 'Our Father' with her, I kept saying the words as I left her; I know that she did so also. I am certain that we both managed to complete it nine times.

I was cloaked and hooded[81] and handed over to the executioners; I was moved towards the Old Marketplace where the burning was to occur.

My last thoughts were of course of Jehanne. She stood there trembling. I know that she was overcome by my sacrifice, but she also knew that there was no other outcome possible.

She would be ushered onwards by Pierre Cauchon, another dozen meters or so where she would be met by two horsemen, who would lift her up and ride away with her to Luxembourg. Jean de Luxembourg would keep his promise.

The eyes of the crowd followed me. I had arrived at my moment of sacrifice. I was willingly attached to the stake; the dry kindling was soon burning briskly and I was about to be overcome by the smoke I inhaled.

A hush came over the crowd. I prayed aloud:
'Heavenly Father, I praise Thy Name, and come to Thee now.

Holy Mary, Mother of God, pray for me now, my Spirit rises to You.

I began to pray the 'Our Father' again, but only managed to get through it once, instead of my customary nine times. As I prayed, I had a fleeting thought of my mother... on her death bed she had prophesied fire....

====================

As Catharine had foretold, Christine composed her final work, the Hymn to Jeanne d'Arc:

---

[81] Anyone burnt at the stake would have been covered with a bag-like hood, so that their identity could not be seen.

"You who are a young maid
To whom God gives the strength and the power
To be the Champion, and she
Who gives to France the breast
Of peace and sweet nourishing milk,
And to overthrow the rebels,
Truly you see an extraordinary thing!
What an honour for the feminine sex!
It's clear that God loves them."

This was the sign promised by Catharine to Pierre Cauchon.

====================

Life amongst the royal personages continued much as before.

On the 17th November 1431, nine-year-old Henry was crowned Henry VI of England and Henry II of France at the Cathedral of Notre Dame in Paris, by the Cardinal of Winchester. Isabeau had the good sense not to attend.

The actual reign of Henry was short-lived. The next year, Philippe le Bon, the Duc de Bourgogne, was deeply angered by the actions of the Duke of Bedford who married Jacqueline de Luxembourg very soon after the death of Anne, his previous wife, who was the sister of Philippe. Philippe lost all feeling of loyalty to the English crown. He sought out Charles VII, and decided to do his utmost to restore the true French king to the French crown. The people were behind him; they were dissatisfied to be ruled by the English. He took on the task of mediating, instead of confronting.

Resolution occurred because Philippe recognised that Charles VII had not himself borne any responsibility for the death of his father, Jean sans Peur. Philippe accepted Charles VII as his true king. He was fully restored to power. Henry was returned to England.

====================

Jehanne retreated from public life as required. She married le Comte Robert des Armoises on the 25th August 1436 at a Church in Pulligny (between Metz and Saint-Die) in Moselle. She died in 1449 and was buried at the same Church[82].

====================

If La Pucelle de France died a Saint in the 15th Century, why did her Canonisation not occur until the 20th?

---

[82] Source: Pierre de Sermoise: JEANNE D'ARC ET LA MANDRAGORE and LES MISSIONS SECRETES DE JEHANNE LA PUCELLE.

Chapter XXX

Epilogue

- December 2001 -

*'God be merciful unto us, and bless us
And cause his face to shine upon us.'*[83]

Catharine is gone now. Her familiar musty scent has disappeared. She no longer interrupts my sleep. My dreams are my own, no longer filled with her persistent stories. I trust that she has finally found her rest. She left me as she promised to do.

And I have been her scribe, as I promised.

Catharine's story challenges the conceit of historians, the myth perpetrated by the Church, the view of tradition, and the accepted 'truth'.

I think I believe her truth now.

===================

---

[83] Psalm 67

Appendix

ROYAL LIVES

King Charles V born in 1338 died in 1380

Queen Jeanne de Bourbon born in 1338 died in 1377

King Charles VI born in 1368 died in 1422
Ascended to the throne at the death of his father in 1380.

Queen Isabeau de Bavière born in 1371 died in 1435

Children of Isabeau and Charles VI

Charles was born in 1386 and died at the age of 2 months, at Vincennes.

Jeanne was born on 14 June 1388 at St Ouen; she died in January 1390.

Isabelle de France was born on 9 November 1389 at the Palais de Louvre. She died on 13 September 1409 in childbirth. Isabelle married Richard II of England (engagement on 12 March 1396, marriage on 4 November 1396). She went to London at the age of seven. Later, in 1406, after the death of Richard II, she married Charles d'Orléans (son of Louis d'Orléans and Valentina Visconti).

Jeanne was born on 24 January 1391 at Mélun. She died on 20 November 1433. She officially married Jean VI de Montfort (son of the duc de Bretagne) on 2 December 1396.(Isabeau began her confinement for Jeanne's birth in August 1390 at St Germaine en Laye.)

Charles was born on 6 February 1392 at l'Hôtel St-Pôl; he died on 13 January 1401.

Children of Isabeau and probably Louis d'Orléans

Marie was born on 22 August 1393 at Vincennes. She was given to the convent at Poissy at the age of 5. She was to be dedicated to God as a sacrifice for Charles' VI sanity. She eventually became the Prioress at Poissy. She died on 19 August 1438.

Michelle was born on 12 January 1395 at l'Hôtel St-Pôl. She married Philippe le Bon (son of Philippe le Hardi) de Bourgogne in 1403. She died on 8 July 1422. She had been poisoned.

Children of Isabeau and Louis d'Orléans

Louis, duc de Guyenne was born on 22 January 1397 at l'Hôtel St-Pôl. He married Marguerite de Bourgogne (daughter of Jean Sans Peur) in 1412. He died on 18 December 1415, silently killed by the conspiracy of his mother Isabeau and Bois-Bourdon. Her reason for seeking his demise was her suspicion that he was a homosexual and would never father children. She had proposed this murder to Jean Sans Peur previously, but he would not comply. He did try to reclaim his daughter's dowry after the death of his son-in-law, but the King was unable to repay it.

Jean was born on 31 August 1398 at l'Hôtel St-Pôl. He married Jacqueline de Bavière daughter of William IV de Bavière and Marguerite de Bourgogne (sister of Jean Sans Peur) in 1406. In 1414 he became Duc de Touraine; he became Dauphin in 1415, also took the titles Comte de Poitou and Duc de Berri. He died in April 1417, the result of another murder conspiracy between Isabeau and Bois-Bourdon.

Catherine was born on 27 October 1401 at l'Hôtel St-Pôl. She married Henry V of England at Troyes Cathedral in June 1420 (Queen of England from 1420 – 1422, then Queen Mother of Henry VI, until her death). Subsequently she married Owen

Tudor and had two sons with him, Edmund and Jasper. She died on 3 June 1438.

Charles VII was born (of political necessity) at l'Hôtel St-Pôl on 22 February 1403. He married Marie d'Anjou. He became duc de Touraine when Jean became Dauphin; he became Dauphin in 1417, Regent in 1418, was crowned King at Reims in 1429. He died on 22 July 1461.

Jehanne[1] was born 7 November 1407. She was officially burnt at the stake in 1431. She got married to Robert des Armoises in 1436. She died in 1449.

---

[1] officially called Philippe and officially born dead on the 10th November. Authentic court records from the 22nd August 1407 until the beginning of July 1408 are missing. Official court records were inserted later; written on paper not produced until 1448 (proven by water mark difference). All royal personages have always been interred at St Denis; after the French Revolution (in 1793) all remains were exhumed. No record of any child Philippe, nor any coffin which would have carried his remains, was ever found.

Children of Charles VI and Odette Champdivert (La Petite Reine)

Two daughters, one given the title:

Marguerite de Valois

Louis, Duc d'Orléans   born 1370   died on 23 November 1407

Valentina Visconti   born 1371   died in November 1408

Children of Valentina Visconti and Louis, Duc d'Orléans

Charles d'Orléans was born in November 1393. He married Isabelle de France in 1406; she died in childbirth in 1409. After, in 1410 he married Bonne d'Armagnac. He was imprisoned in England after Agincourt from October 1415 until 1422. Afterwards, he married Marie de Clèves and with her had a son who became Louis XII, succeeding his (heirless) uncle Louis XI. He died in 1465.

Marie was born in 1396. She was betrothed to Louis, duc de Guyenne, but the marriage was not allowed by the Church.

Philippe became the Comte de Vertus, married a daughter of Jean sans Peur, died in 1420.

Jean de Valois was born in 1399. He became the Comte d'Angoulême; he was an Ancestor of François I. He died in 1468.

Child of Louis, Duc d'Orléans and mistress Mariette d'Enghien

Jehan, Comte de Dunois, the Bastard of Orléans was born on 23 November 1402. He was looked after by Valentina in his early years. He was raised with Charles VII until the age of 10. He was knighted in 1423.

Children of Christine de Pisan and Etienne de Castel

Marie de Castel, born in 1381, became a nun at Poissy

Jean de Castel, became notary to Charles VI (1409-1418) married Jehannette Cotton, daughter of another royal secretary. They had three children born between 1413 and 1418.

The third child was a son; he died at an early age.

CHARLES VI'S EPISODES OF MADNESS

There were 44 attacks, each lasting 3 – 9 months, from 1392 until his death in 1422. There were intervals of sanity, lasting 3 – 6 months in between.[2]

Some further specific dates of madness were:

- June 1393 – January 1394

- August 1395 – February 1396

- late December 1396 / January 1397 – July 1397

- From the late Spring 1398, Charles was ill, off and on, so that it was difficult to assess clearly the state of his health at any given time. He was well enough to convene a meeting for the purpose of ending the Great Schism in 1398.

- He was pronounced incurable in 1400.

From 1402 the Queen made visits to Charles around the time that she knew herself to be pregnant, so that a guise of legitimacy around the births of her children could be maintained.

May 1402 Isabeau presented herself to Charles, and her presence initiated a further bout of madness.

He was clearly distressed (and sane) when he discovered in 1408 that he had officially forgiven Jean Sans Peur for the murder of his brother Louis (at a moment when he was not sane).

Charles was mostly mad, but had good moments of lucidity, in particular when Isabeau was absent from him. One such moment occurred in 1417 when Charles took charge of the situation with Bois-Bourdon.

---

[2] We have correlated Charles VI's periods of madness with the times when Isabeau's children must have been conceived to make the determinations of paternity.

THE PAPACY, 1376 ONWARDS....

Avignon	**Rome**	**Itinerant/Hidden**
1376 Gregory XI -------->	1377-78 Gregory XI	
1378-94 Clement VII	1378-89 Urban VI	
1394-1423 Benedict XIII (Pedro de Luna)	1389-1404 Boniface IX	
•	1404-06 Innocent VII	
•	1406-15 Gregory XII	1409-10 Alexander V
•		1410-15 John XXIII
•	1415-17 NO ROMAN POPES	
1423-1429 Clement VIII	1417-31 Martin V	1425-29 Benedict XIV[3]
	1431-47 Eugenius	
	1447-55 Nicholas V	

---

[3] Jean Carrière, sponsored by the Duc d'Armagnac
The Duc d'Armagnac wrote a letter to Jehanne in 1429 requesting that she, with her divine guidance, determine which of the three popes was the true representative of Saint Peter.

# *About the Authors*

         Anna De Feo   Kenane Barlow

Kenane Barlow was born in 1930, of a French mother and a Scottish-Russian father. She spent her early life in Egypt, and arrived in England on V-E Day 1945. She was educated in a convent school in England, returned to Egypt in 1949, and travelled extensively, lived in Paris in 1951-52, returning to the United Kingdom in 1954 where she married in 1955. She separated from her husband in 1969 and brought up her five children on her own. She and her husband reconciled in the late 1980s and they again lived together from 1994 until his death in 1997. Kenane's life experiences and her imagination, and her fascination with medieval France have fuelled her passion to write this book. Kenane currently resides in Fulham, London

Anna De Feo was born in 1945 in Stamford, Connecticut of a Swedish mother and a Norwegian father. She grew up on Long Island, New York. She spent the year 1964-65 teaching school in Norway, studied briefly in Paris, and completed degrees in New York: BA in Mathematics, MBA in Management, MS in Banking. She married in 1970 and has two children. She spent most of her career working in banking and then in consulting, frequently travelling on assignment throughout Latin America and Europe. She currently travels a great deal with her husband. She resides with him both in Fulham, London and in Garden City, New York. Anna is responsible for channelling the shared creativity into a logical whole.

Kenane and Anna met in Bishops Park, London, by the Thames, where Anna jogged for health and Kenane walked her two Westies, Sam and Max. It was here that they began their discussions that led to this surprising collaboration.

Printed in the United States
1435600002B/1-12